Confessions of A First Lady 2

By:

Denora M. Boone

As always dedicated to my mother and father Dorothy and Fred Jefferson. I pray you are both proud of the woman I have become. Please keep watching over us.

Acknowledgements

No one deserves my praise more than God Himself. It is because of Him that I am on my fourth book and has had the success that I have been given. I'm so thankful that He saw something in me that I never saw in myself, and I am able to bring a message from Him through the stories I write. God I thank you.

Every woman thinks they have the best husband in the world, but I know that I have been given that gift. Byron, you are an amazing man of God and I love and adore you because of that very fact. You continue to push me and guide me, never leaving me to handle things on my own. No matter what glitch was thrown in our matrix that we call life, you kept your head held high and stood strong. I appreciate you more than you will know and I'm thankful that our children have such an awesome man that they call Daddy in their lives.

My children mean everything to me; even when they are misbehaving they bring me so much joy. The smile I see on their faces each time they say they love me or they are proud of me, makes me that much more determined to provide them with the best life possible. They are my little prayer warriors and I love you all.

I told my sisters that each and every book that I write, they will have a space in my acknowledgements. Not because we are family, but because each and every day they show me how much they really love me, flaws and all. Krystal Sheppard and

Deja McCullough, no matter what we go

through in life, the both of you have been

right here beside me through it all. People

would think we grew up in the same

household all of our lives the way we are

with one another, because our bond is just

that unbreakable. I thank you for

continuing to be my pudds!

There are so many people who have

come into my life in this past year that

make me realize just how blessed I am. My

publisher David Weaver, I know you get

tired of me thanking you on the regular but I can't help it, because you have opened a door of blessings for my family and I that you didn't have to. Thank you from the bottom of my heart. Now let's make this movie!

To everyone that reps #TBRS, from the heart, I thank you. We stand strong together through it all and you all have welcomed me into this family with opened arms. No judgment, just unconditional love. I love each of you!

Now let's see what shenanigans First

Lady and Iesha are up to now shall we?

Love,

Dee

Last time.....

Marcus

I couldn't believe what I was seeing and hearing as I stood frozen in place. Two of my members lay dead in the middle of our church, and my wife's former lover is crazy, deranged and still continuing to reveal secrets about Veronica's past. The moment the older couple walked in the door, it instantly reminded me that our children were still outside. Or were they? Had this psycho done something to them, because two shots were already fired and no one had run inside.

I prayed that they were safe and if they were, they were trying to get us some help. I thought my prayer had been answered and that help had come by way of Officer Norman, as she walked into the church right behind the couple. But I quickly put that theory to rest as she walked past everyone, right up to the front, and gave a quick kiss to Iesha.

"Oh, I'm sorry, how rude of me. This is Adrian. Officer Adrian Norman," Iesha said, showing all of her teeth and beaming with pride.

"Iesha baby, what are you doing?" said the older woman who I learned was her mother. "Did you do all of this? Oh my God, Iesha, did you kill these people?" she said running up to Iesha, but stopped dead in her tracks as Iesha pointed her gun directly between her mother's eyes.

At that moment, I think everyone was holding their breaths. We didn't know if she was going to kill Mrs. Verna, her own mother, or if she was going to allow her to live.

"Please don't do this. We can try and fix this. Don't hurt anyone else," Mrs. Verna pleaded. You could hear the weariness in her voice and knew this was a long battle that she was tired of fighting against her daughter.

"Oh mother, always trying to be the peace maker. Mrs. Fixer Upper, if you will."

"Why do you have to keep doing this? Can't you see Veronica is happy with her family and she doesn't want you anymore? This may be your reality but this isn't hers," spoke her father for the first time since entering the church.

"You've done enough harm by outing her to their congregation, and God knows how many other people. Please just let it go." Mrs. Verna was now crying as Adrian and Iesha looked at each other as if they were the only ones in the room. They were speaking to each other only through their eyes. No words. Then they turned towards me.

"Well mommy dearest, since I have already exposed Veronica, how much fun would it be to expose someone else?" Iesha asked nonchalantly. Although she was speaking to her mother, she was looking me dead in my eyes.

"Iesha, what are you talking about? What have you done?" her father asked.

"Oh not me," she said shrugging and nodding her head towards me. "Him."

"Me?!" I said not knowing what she was talking about. At that moment, I noticed a remote in her hand as she turned on the projector behind me.

There was the back of my chair, facing the hidden camera that had been placed in my office, and Adrian could be seen just as clear as day unbuttoning her uniform top. She disappeared from the view in front of the chair and I could be heard mumbling.

I dropped my head in shame.

"Looks like First Lady isn't the only one with confessions, huh Pastor?" Iesha said before my world went black.

Chapter *One*

Marcus

I sat back in my chair behind the pulpit as the youth leader announced the next dance group, Divine Praises. They consisted of our thirteen to seventeen-year-old young ladies in the church, and our daughters Destiny and Dynasty were amongst them.

I watched closely as the girls got into position, and couldn't help but to smile at my daughters. After all of the trials and tribulations that we have gone through the last six months, I was amazed at how well they were handling all of the changes. There were some days though, that I could see the weariness on their little young faces; but for the most part, they were holding it together pretty well.

I looked over to my left into a face that resembled mine so much that it sometimes scared me. Looking at my sixteen-year-old son MJ, who was now the proud father of a beautiful little girl, Cadence Noel Millhouse, it seemed like he had grown into a man overnight. Well I guess he kind of had to. Although his mother and I were disappointed in his actions, we never wanted him to feel like we were disappointed in *him.* Those were two separate things and we would never make our children feel like they were less than all, because of the mistakes they had made or would make in the future. They would never feel like they would have to go to anyone else for help or to talk to, before they came to us. That just wouldn't sit well with me. No we are not our children's friends, but they trust us enough to know that they can come to us no matter what the circumstance may be.

Us. Not sure if there really is an *"us"* anymore, as in Veronica and myself; but before I could dwell on that too much, the intro to Tasha Cobb's version of "For Your Glory" began to play, and I focused on my girls and the joy they were

about to bring to God during this performance.

"Lord if I
Find favor in Your sight
Lord please
Hear my heart's cry

I'm desperately waiting
To be where You are.
I'll cross the hottest desert
I'll travel near or far

For Your glory
I will do anything
Just to see You
To behold You as my King

For Your glory
I will do anything
Just to see You
To behold You as my King

I wanna be where You are
I gotta be where You are
I wanna be where You are
I gotta be where You are

I wanna be where You are
Gotta be where You are
I wanna be where You are
Gotta be where You are"

By the time the girls had finished performing, there wasn't a dry eye in the house. Sure the congregation had gotten a little smaller over the last few months, but that didn't stop the presence of God from falling fresh on each one of the people that filled this space right now.

I couldn't stop the tears from falling down my face, but right now I didn't want them to. I was always a believer in tears being our liquid prayers to God, when words couldn't be formulated in order to cry out to Him. So, I just let them fall on the outside while I was cleansed from the inside. As I made my way over to the pulpit and looked out at everyone worshiping, there was something lacking inside of me and I missed the feeling of completion my life used to have.

"My God," I started, but the lump in my throat was the size of a boulder. I took a few seconds to compose myself before speaking again, and before I could open my mouth I heard the word *"release"* and knew at that moment, God was speaking to me telling me to give it to him.

Opening my mouth I began to sing the song that came to my spirit.

"When your spirit speaks to me with my whole heart I'll agree and my answer will be yes Lord yes! I'll say yes Lord yes to your will and to your way, I'll say yes Lord yes I will trust you and obey. When your spirit speaks to me with my whole heart I'll agree. And my answer will be yes Lord yes!"

"It's alright Pastor! It's gonna be alright," Malachi said coming to stand by my side. This man has really been my support system and best friend during the darkest time in our lives. Honestly, if it hadn't been for him and his wife Torre, I wouldn't be standing behind this pulpit this Sunday, bringing a word from God.

It had been almost six months since the destruction that took place in this very building, and I didn't think I had it in me to continue to do the work God had assigned me to do. For a while it just didn't seem worth it. We spend all of our time doing our best to walk with Christ, just to get beat down with one trial after the next.

I had wanted to give it all up because I felt like God had given me and my family up to the enemy, with no regards as to how much we loved Him and worshiped Him. But it was

Malachi and Torre who were praying when I couldn't, and encouraging me, even when I just wished they would be quiet.

It was Malachi that helped me to remember that in order for us to get to where God wants us to be, He has to take us through the storms of life. The more he talked, the more I thought about all that Jesus had endured before He got up on that cross for me, and nothing that I was going through was nearly as bad as that; although it may have felt like it.

I understood what he was saying to me and knew that no matter what it looked like, I couldn't turn my back on the one who has never turned His back on me. So, here I am

months later about to give a sermon that I

prayed would not just minister to the people,

but to me as well. I was in need of a

breakthrough.

I gave him a nod to let him know that I was

okay to proceed, and he took his seat again

beside his wife, as she held our beautiful

granddaughter in her arms.

"Didn't our youth do a wonderful job?" I

asked the congregation. Although I had this

message prepared, I was stalling. At this

moment something in me didn't want to give

this word today and I felt like I had to address

what was really going on in my life. I had to be as transparent as I possibly could and I had honestly been avoiding the issue. I didn't know where to begin, but prayer always seemed to be the best answer for everything.

"Let us pray," I said, bowing my head as everyone in the building did the same.

"Heavenly father, we come to you with closed eyes and heavy hearts first to thank you for allowing us another day to even open our eyes and come to your house and fellowship with one another. Now God, before we ask of any request from you, we ask for your forgiveness. Forgiveness father, for each and every sin that we have committed known and unknown. No matter how small and insignificant we may think they are, we understand that they still stink in your nostrils.

God, help us to be able to focus on the calling that you have put on each and every one of our lives and accept the things that you are asking us to change in order for us to be better. Lord, we ask that you meet the needs of everyone that is under the sound of my voice and bring comfort and peace to us all.

We never know why it is that you do the things that you do, but help us to continue to have faith in you to carry out what is best for us. Now God, I pray for families, all families that are going through some of the worst times in their lives, especially mine. I trust you, God that all things will work together for our good, even if we don't see it right now. We know that with you all things are possible and we ask right now of you to fix it. Heal our broken hearts and ease our troubled minds and we will be so gracious as to give you all of the honor, all of the glory, and all of the praise in Jesus' mighty name we pray, Amen."

As I opened my eyes, I took a deep breath and became transparent.

Chapter *Two*

Iesha

I am in heaven! Not literally, because we all know I'm not bout that life. When it's my time to go, I'm sure I'll be busting hell wide open and screaming, "TURN UP! TURN UP! TURN UP!" as I take my place on that fiery throne next to Satan. It's cool though. I have finally come to terms with my life and all of the things I have done during my time here, but none of that matters anymore now that I'm with the love of my life.

I was laying in one of the most luxurious suites that the Jumeirah Beach Hotel in Dubai, had to offer. We were staying in the Royal Ocean Suite that faced the famous Burj Al Arab Hotel, the clear blue waters of the Arabian Gulf, and a beach with sand so white you would think it was snow if it wasn't for the warm weather.

The room reminded me of how the inside of Jeanie's genie lamp looked in one of my favorite shows as a kid "I Dream of Jeanie." It had a huge round king-sized bed that faced the private sun terrace that we had, overlooking the water. The décor was bright and vibrant. Lots of reds, pinks, gold, and light blue splashed around the room. We had a separate living room with an "L" shaped sectional and a seventy-inch flat screen mounted on the wall, if we wanted to kick back and watch TV, with some of the softest carpet known to man throughout the room.

And don't let me get started on the bathroom! If I could live in there I would. The tub was big enough to fit at least six people in, and sat at the back of the room by the window with a view so breathtaking, I had to pause each time I walked in there.

I could get used to living like this. Traveling the world to exotic locations and staying in five star resorts was just what the doctor ordered for a girl like me. I had been held captive so long by doing what everyone else wanted, that I had yet to live for myself. Well it was my time now, and I was about to have the time of my life!

I looked over to my left as Adrian stirred in her sleep and her hair fell over her face. I couldn't lie... she was beautiful; and after the way she handled the whole situation with Veronica, I knew she was a rider.

Never did she have any back talk for me when I told her what I needed her to handle and quite frankly, had it not been for her, I would be in jail right now for those two murders I committed months ago.

She was definitely my "ram in the bush" as y'all church folks called it. Adrian had enough information on everyone in that sanctuary to cause their worlds to be turned upside down; even more than I had, if they uttered a word as to who was responsible for lying to rest those holy rollers.

I wish y'all could have seen them. The looks of disgust and fear that was plastered all over each of their faces, gave me a high like no other! It was something about being in control and having that power over them that made me almost have a…well you know. I don't have to even explain that one. Needless to say, life was good.

I started to get out of the bed so that I could get a few moments of alone time, before we got out to enjoy the day. I eased myself down to the floor, not wanting to disturb her sleep, and made my way over to the terrace. Sliding the patio door open, I was immediately hit with the warm sun and a cool breeze. The weather was so nice here, and I couldn't wait to see everything this place had to offer.

While I was taking in the scenery, I could feel her presence come up behind me. I knew once I was out of the bed she wouldn't be too far behind. It was always hard for us to stay asleep if the other wasn't in the bed beside us. Just something about hearing her heartbeat, and feeling her take every breath, gave me a sense of calm.

I felt her move closer to me and wrap me in her arms. The warmth of her breath on my neck sent a chill through my body and caused a smile to spread across my face.

"Good morning beautiful," I said, still grinning like a Cheshire cat, or "Chester cat" as the old folks say. For them to be so old and wise they sure were dumb.

"Hey baby. I haven't felt this good in a long time. You really worked me over."

"Well it's all about you. Do you have in mind what you want to do today?" I asked, still looking out over the water.

"I don't want to venture out too far today. Although it's been a while since I've been on vacation here, I just want to relax around here, go to the spa and get the works, you know? I missed how the air and the water smelled here," she said, taking a sniff of the fresh air and smiling, but I could see there was something on her mind.

"Babe what's wrong?" I asked her. After everything that has been going on, the last thing I wanted was for anything to be bothering her. This was supposed to be our getaway and I refused to let anyone or anything ruin it.

"Huh? Oh nothing. Let's just stay here a few more minutes before we get dressed. Then we can get this day started," she said kissing me. I didn't believe a word she was saying, but I would let it ride for now. I would be watching her closely because although I loved her, I didn't completely trust her as far as I could throw her.

Chapter *Three*

Adrian

I had been up for hours, but I remained as still as possible so that Iesha would think I was still sleeping. I wanted to see if she would do or say anything crazy because while I was here with her, I knew I didn't have a hundred percent of her. And in order to carry out this little plan of my own that I had, I needed to make sure she was putty in my hands. That would be a little difficult though, but I was up for the challenge.

Iesha turned to face me and although I had my eyes closed, I knew she was staring at me. That's something that she often did while I slept. Being a police officer, well ex-police officer, I knew how to play things off and while she thought that I was sound asleep, I was wide awake, waiting on her next move. I learned to be able to see with my ears if that makes any sense. My ears became my eyes many times when I couldn't see a suspect, so I had to be able to hear their location. I was a pro at this now. I knew exactly what she was doing without even opening my eyes, as she slid out of the bed and stepped out on the terrace.

I lay there a few more minutes reminiscing on how things all started almost two years ago, and I smiled inwardly.

Knock. Knock.

"Enter," was all that came from the other side of the door, as I opened it and stepped in. My superior, Detective Patrick Johansen, had just been transferred to the force only a short while ago; two or three months at the most. He was arrogant and cocky and no one really cared too much for him. But I thought the Chi-town swag

gave the short white man a little sex appeal. Not much, but some.

"You wanted to see me, sir?" I asked, still standing by the door.

"Have a seat, Officer," he said, never looking up from the pictures that were before him on his desk.

I sat down and waited for him to explain to me why he had me in his office. I hadn't done anything out of line and my performance at work was impeccable.

"Who is this?" he asked, as he slid one of the pictures over to me.

I sat up in my chair and reached out for the photo. It was one of First Lady Veronica Millhouse that was taken during a Sunday service over at Clover Hill Church of God In Christ.

"This is the First Lady of the church I started attending," I said, handing it back to him.

I hoped that my outward appearance was showing that I was calm and collected, because on the inside I felt like I was about to throw up. The last thing I needed was for my cover to be blown. I wasn't on an assignment from the force; this assignment was a personal one.

"How well do you know this First Lady, as you call her?" he asked me. The tone in his voice was telling me that he was aware of something that I didn't want anyone to know just yet.

"I have only gone to that church a handful of times with my aunt and my friend. I haven't officially met her," I said, hoping that this line of questioning would come to an end.

"Humph," he grunted, like he could read right through me, as he stared into my eyes. I'm sure he saw me shaking like a stripper, but I wasn't about to cave.

Sliding another picture over to me, he kept quiet this time, as he held my attention with his gaze. I didn't look down as I picked it up off of his desk, and when I did my heart stopped. I knew I was busted and had no idea how I was going to get out of this one. If the reason I was here came out, I'm sure I would lose my job.

"Sir, I can explain," I started, only to be stopped by him.

"No need. Seems as though we are both on a mission and can help each other," he said, picking up the phone on his desk and instructing someone to come to his office.

I didn't know who would be walking into that office and truth be told, I was scared out of my mind. Before I had time to wreck my brain trying to figure it out, in walked a blast from the past.

"This is Officer Adrian Norman. Norman, this is-" he started his introduction when I cut him off.

"Iesha, long time no see," I said as Detective Johansen looked on with a bewildered look on his face. Obviously, whatever little plan he had, he hadn't done all of his homework because if he had, he would have known that Iesha and I had history.

It had been so long since we had seen one another, and I knew if she was here in Atlanta, then we were both on the same mission. Veronica "Ronnie" Millhouse.

"It's good to see you, Adrian. It's been a while," she said, as she walked around the desk to Patrick and sat on his lap.

I'm sure the look on my face said everything I was thinking, because it caused them both to laugh out loud. I didn't catch the punch line and I sat waiting on someone to tell me what in the world was going on.

"Don't look so surprised, boo. I brought us together since we have the same agenda," Iesha said, giving me a knowing look.

I should have known that this would eventually happen, but I had hoped to take care of this situation with Veronica on my own. I guess *this would be a team effort the way that Johansen was lusting after Iesha's body. This girl had no shame and little did he know, he was holding the short end of the stick.*

The giggling that I heard on the terrace brought me back to the present and caused me to open my eyes. Instantly, I felt like I was on fire, as I watched the scene play out before me. No matter what I did to help Iesha, she would never love me like that. I guess they felt me staring out at them, but instead of locking eyes with the woman that meant so much to me, I focused my sight on my sister, Veronica.

Chapter *Four*

Marcus

Standing in the window looking out into our backyard, I felt so empty on the inside. My house no longer felt like a home with Veronica not there. No matter what we had gone through, if she was to walk back in this house right now, all would be forgiven. The kids missed their mother so much and I heard Dez cry and pray for her mother every night. It broke my heart because even though I would go to the ends of the earth for my children and I was a good father, I couldn't teach my daughters how to be women. They needed their mother and I knew that no matter where she was, she needed us too.

I don't know what was going on in Veronica's mind the day she ran out of the church, as the video of Officer Norman in my office with me, played on the projection screen. I remember wondering where my children were while everything was going down, because they hadn't come inside. I was so scared that something had happened to them and just wanted to see their faces, but once I heard my moans coming through the speakers, I prayed fervently that they wouldn't walk in. We were all dealing with so much and this was the last thing that I needed for them to see.

As soon as I realized what was going on in that office, I looked over at Veronica to see fresh tears free falling down her beautiful, brown cheeks. God in heaven knows at that moment, seeing the hurt and pain this caused her, broke my heart. I prided myself on being a faithful husband, and almost twenty years later, I had never stepped out on my wife. Technically, I still hadn't, as I thought back to that day.

About two weeks before everything went down at the church Veronica was still on bed rest and we had a counseling session with, who we now knew as Officer Adrian Norman and her fiancé Keith. The two wanted me to marry them since they had recently joined the church, but I never married anyone without having at least four sessions with them.

Veronica was in no way, shape, or form, able to make it to this one, so I was going to have our liaison, Jonah, sit in for her. If I was meeting with anyone in my office for anything, I always had someone else present, especially if there was a woman there. With so much going on, you could never be too careful. The last thing I needed was for someone to say that I said or did something to them behind closed doors. It would *be their words against mine, and no matter what*

title I held in church, I was still a man.

I'd arrived an hour early because I wanted

to read over their questionnaire that we had

everyone fill out beforehand. It was always good

to have an idea of what to pray about and how to

help them, if I could meditate over it first. Trying

to make sure that everyone at home was okay, it

had slipped my mind to bring it home with me the

other day, so that Veronica could read over it with

me.

By the information that they had filled out,

you would think that they had the perfect

relationship, but we all knew that looks were

very deceiving. Right as I was finishing up, Jonah came over the intercom to let me know that Adrian and Keith had arrived.

"Come in," I said, standing to greet them as Jonah walked into the room, followed by the soon-to-be newlyweds.

"Good morning Pastor," Keith said, as he reached his hand out to shake mine.

"Good to see you son. How are you today, Adrian?" I asked, shaking her hand as well.

"I'm fine Pastor. Thank you for meeting with us," she said, but there was something that wasn't right now that I had the two of them in my presence at the same time. I had always talked to them separately, and even though they came to church together, they never sat beside one another or interacted with each other, until they were heading out.

Veronica had always said that there was something strange yet familiar about Adrian, and I agreed. We just couldn't think of what it was. The day of the accident when she came to the hospital, she was polite and very professional but even then, just a tad bit strange. I shook it off due to everything that was going on around us, and didn't dwell on it too much.

"Since First Lady isn't able to join us today, I have Jonah sitting in to take notes and if needed, give a married woman's point of view. If you are ready, let's go ahead and open with a word of prayer," I said, as everyone nodded and bowed their heads.

"Lord, we come to you this morning asking for guidance and understanding on all matters brought before you on this day for this couple. Lord, you say in your word in Proverbs, chapter eighteen and verse twenty two, that he who finds a wife finds a good thing and obtains favor from the Lord. Let this session be one of confirmation

and understanding on the issues and challenges they may face going forward. Amen."

"Amen," everyone in the room said. I usually don't end a prayer as abruptly as I did that one, but something wasn't right. God wouldn't allow me to go any further so I had to end it there. What was going on? I wondered before I started.

"So first things first, how long have the two of you been together?" I asked.

"Two years," Adrian said.

"A year," said Keith at the same time.

I'm sure the look on my face was one of complete confusion but I said nothing. The truth always came out.

*"Well, you know how women are, Pastor,"
Keith began with a nervous laugh. "She counts from the time we met and I count from the time we made it official."*

"Hmm. Yeah, women do find those little things important while us men not so much," I said, trying my best to not feel whatever it was that was vexing my spirit.

"Are there any issues that you want to specifically discuss that wasn't on your questionnaire? I noticed that everything looked

to be perfect, but we all know that's not the case in any relationship. Even something that you may think is small now may become something bigger as the years go on," I continued.

"Um well," Adrian started out. It looked like she was trying to make up something to talk about while Keith sat there looking nervous as ever. What was going on here? Before any of us could go forward, my cell phone rang and so did the phone that Jonah carried with her, when she was away from her desk.

I normally would turn my cell off while in a session, but because Veronica was at home, I needed to make sure I was available to her and our children if there was an emergency.

"Would you please excuse me? This is First Lady calling and I need to make sure she is okay," I said standing to my feet. It could have been my imagination, but I could have sworn that Adrian rolled her eyes after I said Veronica was on the phone. I didn't have time to figure that one out, as both Jonah and I excused ourselves to take the calls.

It was strange that my wife was calling because she knew that I was in a session, so I hoped that everything was okay with her.

"Hey baby, is everything okay?" I asked with a little panic in my voice.

"Well I don't know. Have you started speaking with Adrian and Keith yet?" she asked, sounding like something was bothering her.

"We haven't gotten in too deep yet, but something does seem a little off between the two of them and I'm not sure what that is," I said being open with her.

"Hmm," was all she said in response to what I had just told her.

"Babe what's wrong?" I asked. I knew my wife very well, and when there was something heavy on her mind she couldn't hide it.

"It's just that I was taking a nap and had this dream that Adrian and Keith aren't who they say they are. I mean, their names are real, but I don't think the relationship is," she said. I knew she thought I would probably not believe what she was saying, but little did she know I had my own suspicions. Instead of her worrying, I told her it was probably just the medications causing her to have these dreams and that I would do my best to hurry this session along so I could come home.

Walking back into my office, I saw that Jonah hadn't returned and it looked like Adrian and Keith had been in a heated discussion in my absence.

"I apologize. Veronica needed me to pick up a new prescription for her on my way home," I lied. God forgive me for that.

"Oh it's fine. Would you excuse me please, Pastor, I need to use the restroom if that's okay," Keith said, before standing to exit.

"Sure son, go ahead. Jonah will be back in a few minutes," I said taking a sip of my water. God knows a glass of wine would do me some good right now for this stress I was dealing with. Or

even a glass of Hennessey, but I knew that was stretching it a little. The Bible does say "Drink ye all of it." I'm kidding; that was all out of context of what it meant.

As I laughed at my little joke on the inside, I watched Keith lean in to kiss Adrian on her cheek, and she flinched when he did it. That's odd, I thought.

Adrian sat there with a mischievous smirk on her face, looking right at me. For a split second, it looked like her face became distorted and then went back to normal. I had to shake my head to try and get myself together, but I could feel my body getting heavy and sinking further into my leather high back office chair.

What was going on?

Adrian stood up and headed towards the door. I thought she was going to go get me some help, but instead of opening it and leaving, she locked it. Everything after this point couldn't be good. My eyes were so heavy and getting heavier by the second.

My water. One of them had to have put something in there while they waited for Jonah and me to return, but why?

"Yes I put something in your water," she said, confirming my suspicions when she noticed I was looking at my glass.

Whhhhhyy…wwwhhhhhat's happening?" I slurred.

"Well Pastor, your sweet little wife's past is coming to remind her that she needs to pay up for what she's done. Now I get that everything she has done was before you, but when you haven't paid your debt to the ones you have hurt, you better be ready when the time comes," she said, now standing over me.

"Nooooo Gooood has…has…forgiiivin her."

Talking was getting to be extremely difficult. Where was Keith and Jonah?

It was as if she could read my mind once again when she said, "Keith has little miss Jonah occupied right now. Oh and before I forget, he's not really my fiancé. That dummy thinks that we are undercover to expose you because this church is just a front for the illegal activity that you were doing back in St. Louis."

I didn't know what to say, or rather I couldn't speak. Whatever she had slipped in my water now had me unable to do anything. My eyes were closed, but I could still hear her and feel her turning my chair around, so that the back faced my bookshelf I had in the office.

"You just be still and let me do all of the work. Ha! I guess you have no choice but to do that, huh?" she said more to herself than to me.

"You know what... this uniform is getting a little hot. Mind if I take it off, Marcus?" All formalities were gone out of the window.

I felt something hit my lap, assuming it was her top, and instantly I felt something that I know I shouldn't have, going on down below. "Jesus please help me!" I thought I was saying out loud, but not a sound came out right then; only a moan.

I guess she thought that I was enjoying it, not realizing I was trying to speak.

"I knew you would cave in sooner or later. Now are you ready to make a movie?" she asked, as I mustered up enough energy to pop my eyes open.

"Now relax baby, and let me do all of the work and show you what my sister isn't capable of."

Sister. Who's her sister? What on earth is going on?

Before I could process anything she had just said, I felt her unfasten my pants, as I couldn't keep the sounds from coming from my body. I'm

sure Jesus just wept again.

Fix it Jesus.

Chapter *Five*

Iesha

I knew that Adrian was in her feelings about Veronica being here with me too, but oh well, she would have to get over it. She knew where my heart was and although she was my saving grace, she couldn't hold a candle to Ronnie. Now she knew either she better fall in line with what I want, or she can kick rocks with sandals on.

It didn't take as long as I thought it would to get Veronica back, once she saw the beginning of the video that day. Everything she had known to be true with her husband, came crashing down. Yet again, she took it as another man that she loved unconditionally, hurt her; it caused something in her to snap.

After the death of her father, I knew how she yearned for another man to love her and take care of her the way he did. No matter how messed up his raising of her may have been, that man did love his daughter; he just had a different way of showing it.

Before I had gotten involved with Veronica, I was so in love with my pimp, Bean. He was nowhere near the status of Clarence, Veronica's father. So I came up with a plan to bring him down. I just hadn't planned on getting that close to Veronica, and eventually the love I had for her outweighed my love for Bean. I understood then why Clarence was on top.

In order to pull this off, I needed an accomplice. So one night while working the block, I overheard a conversation between two of the chicks that had just started trickin' for Bean. When I heard one of them mention Veronica and her father, the wheels in my head began to spin and I began plotting.

****

I was sitting on the couch in the living room and making sure that I had everything I needed in my clutch. Earlier, Veronica just wanted to lounge around but later on, we all decided a night out would do us some good. We had been here for a while, and until we got word from Detective Johansen that we were clear to come back to the states, we were going to sit tight.

Trust and believe that he was mad that he got used, but he had not one leg to stand on because I had dirt on him, too, if he wanted to get bubble guts of the mouth. I bet if I went down though, everybody else was going down along with me.

Once I had everything in place, I stood to look at myself in the mirror. The club we were going to had a dress code that everyone must wear white in order to enter. I had to admit that I was looking good tonight. We had taken most of the day to get pampered, and this sew-in I was rocking was laid for the gawds, hunty! My outfit was on point too. I was rocking some white high-waist shorts from Charlotte Russe, a white satin bra that had the girls sitting up nice, a white blazer also from Charlotte Russe, with a bad pair of Christian Dior booties. I turned to the side to admire myself, just as Veronica and Adrian came into the room.

Yes I looked good, but I had no problem saying they would be slaying every woman in the spot tonight. Adrian had her Senegalese twist falling down her back, stopping right above her tail bone. Her look was simple in a white jumpsuit that hugged everything she had to offer, and her face was beat to perfection.

Veronica walked over to the bar that we had inside the suite, and took out three shot glasses and a bottle of vodka. We couldn't read the name, but alcohol is alcohol. As she was pouring up I admired her, because she put both Adrian and myself to shame. Veronica was a size eighteen, easy, but it was all in the right places.

She had on a white halter peplum dress that had a plunging neckline with her back exposed, some crystal encrusted Yves St. Laurent pumps, with her long hair styled in a Mohawk, and the curls cascading down the middle. I knew Marcus was home missing this piece of perfection that he used to have. Now it was my time to enjoy what was mine in the first place.

"Let's ride," she said, after we had taken about six shots a piece and were starting to feel the effects of the liquor. We grabbed our

belongings and were on our way.

****

Walking into the club, you couldn't tell us

anything! There was

no doubt in my mind that we were the flyest

women that stepped in

the club, because the way the men's eyes were

glued to us told us so.

It was so appropriate that the deejay was

playing Ne-Yo's "She Knows" as we headed to

the VIP to get our night started.

If it's one thing I knew about these Saudi

Princes is that they

loved to spend those coins on a beautiful

woman, and who better to

spend it than me and my boos. Adrian had a bad

body and attitude

to go with it. She put a little extra stank on her

walk, as we walked

past the bar and the bouncer lifted the velvet

rope to allow us

access.

Club Arabian was one of the hottest spots

in Dubai. Veronica

hadn't been to a club in so long, but looking at

her rocking to the beat, I knew she was about to

go in. It had taken me way too long to get her

back to her old self, but she was finally there. I

had to pull out my bag of tricks in order loosen

her up but bay bayyy, when I say it was well

worth the wait, trust and believe it felt like old

times. By the time I was done with her, I knew

she didn't remember not one scripture. Shoot,

she probably forgot what a Bible looked like fooling round with me.

We got to our table just as one of the waitresses came over with a bottle of some kind of champagne, that I'm sure wasn't even available in the US. She opened it and poured us each a glass before walking away and telling us to enjoy our evening.

Looking around the crowded room, it was easy to say that this was by far the sexiest club I had ever been to in my life. The whole place was decorated in white, and the black lights gave it that glow. In one section, there was an ice sculpture of the Taj Mahal. Throughout the club were either fluffy white couches or chaise lounges, for the patrons to kick back and relax. With all of this white everywhere and drunken people all over, you would think that everything would be stained from either drinks or food. But surprisingly, everything was crispy white.

When you looked up, there was this crazy huge 3-D art that covered the whole ceiling. It looked like the face was swaying to the music that was beating throughout the building.

"This is nice," Adrian leaned in to say to me.

"Mmm hmm," was my simple reply, while I watched Veronica standing by the railing overlooking the club, with a drink in her hand and swaying her hips to the song playing. The way she was moving was like the way water rippled when it was disturbed; slow and effortlessly.

I could tell Adrian was beginning to get in her feelings, but I couldn't stop watching the show in front of me. It was like she was the only one in the room.

"While you're sitting here gawking at her, you should be over there asking her why she was calling Marcus earlier," Adrian said. Her words laced with malice, and received my undivided attention right away.

"What are you talking about?" I asked, feeling my blood starting to rise. Veronica had told me that she was done with him and even though she missed her kids, she wasn't going to reach out to them. She thought it would be best for the kids and she could care less how Marcus felt.

"I heard her while we were getting dressed. I couldn't hear the full conversation, but it sounded like she was talking to one of her kids and she mentioned his name," Adrian filled me in, with a nonchalant attitude that I knew was just a front. I didn't know she was lying to me right then, but I did know that she was fuming on the inside and it would have made her day to see me spazz out on Veronica.

Instead of saying anything else, I walked over to where she was giving these folks the show of their lives. The deejay was playing Waka's "No Hands" and Veronica was leaving nothing to their imaginations. For a split second, I thought about confronting her with the information that I was just given but decided against it. I was going to wait to see if it happened again and if it did, there would be hell to pay. I could feel Adrian's eyes burning a hole in the back of my head, so I turned around with an expression that said "Try me if you want to". Obviously she got the picture and headed off to the bar to get another bottle. Little did I know, Adrian was about to place a call that would rock everybody's world, especially mine.

Chapter Six

Marcus

As the days went by, it got harder and harder to deal with Veronica being gone. People say that time heals all wounds, but that was definitely not the case in the lives of me and my children. Never in a million years would I have thought this would be my life. Of course I knew there would be trials in life, but come on God, this is a little too much.

Even after Veronica told me about her past, I accepted it and told her we would work things out. I didn't forgive her because quite honestly, she hadn't done anything to me that I had to forgive her for, and God had already forgiven her. If anyone needed to be begging for forgiveness, it should have been Iesha. She's the one that came in and destroyed our family.

"Hey Dad," MJ said, bringing me out of my thoughts. He was standing in the doorway with a crying Cadence in his arms. All of my children were beautiful as babies, but that grandbaby of mine took the cake.

Cadence was my little chocolate drop who had a head full of curly, coal black hair, a dimple on each side of her chubby face, and eyes the color of mahogany. She reminded me of a little porcelain doll, because she was flawless.

"What's wrong with Papa's girl, huh?" I asked, taking the baby out of my son's arms.

"She's been bathed, fed, and burped, and she still won't stop crying," he said looking frustrated.

"Shhhh, it's okay princess," I said, walking around the bed to the window while rocking her gently in my arms.

"How do you do that?" MJ asked me, with a look of confusion on his face.

"Well son, after having three children myself and helping to raise your aunt and uncle, I've learned a few tricks over the years," I said smiling.

"Dad, is she coming back?" he asked me, as I looked up into his weary teenage face.

"I don't know," was all I could say. I honestly didn't have an answer and I didn't want him to get his hopes up. The way things were going, I was starting to lose hope.

"It just doesn't make sense to me. Mom would always tell us how hurt she was that her mother left her, but then she turns around and does it to us?" he said, standing with his arms folded across his chest.

"It makes perfect sense," Dynasty said, entering the room fully. I had no idea she was there listening. I was more surprised that she was actually talking. Although Destiny was the closest to their mother, Dynasty was taking it harder than anyone. She didn't want to be bothered, and most of the time stayed in her room. We all would try and talk to her, but she would just cry.

"What do you mean?" I asked her.

"She's selfish," Dynasty said.

"Man, go 'head with all that, Dy. You know mama put everyone else before herself," MJ said taking up for his mother.

"You mean she put everyone except *me* before her. She never paid the same amount of attention to me as everybody else, and I hope she doesn't come back!" she yelled with tears falling, and ran out of the room.

MJ walked over to me and took his daughter out of my arms, without saying anything further, and left behind her. I was still sitting on the bed, wondering what had just happened and was coming up clueless.

"God, give me the words to say so that my daughter is at peace. I know she didn't mean anything that she just said and its coming from a place of deep hurt. So please allow me to be able to comfort her right now. Her mind and heart are going through conflicting emotions and acting out is the only way that she knows how to cope. Give us a revelation no matter what it may be, and help our family, Lord. We need you. My God, we need you now," I prayed before heading towards Dynasty's bedroom.

Before I had a chance to knock, I heard the weary voice of my daughter singing along with

Marvin Winan's "Just Don't Wanna Know" as she continued to cry.

"Veronica, why did you leave us baby?" I asked the empty hallway, as I continued to listen to my daughter pour her soul out in this song.

"I hurt so many nights, I cried so many hours

Trying to make it right, I just didn't have the power

You ignored all my tears in hopes they'd disappear

I tried to let it show

But I guess you just don't wanna know

I came to you in love, I came to you in earnest

Could you possibly explain?

Oh my, my, why the flames? Why, why the

furnace?

Oh, just needing to get it clear, I was hoping that

you would hear

I tried to let it go

But I guess you just don't wanna know"

I hadn't realized that I had slid down to the floor crying my eyes out, until I felt arms around me. I looked up to find all three of my children, sitting with me with tears in their eyes. It seemed like all we do nowadays is cry; crying for Veronica not being here, crying for each other's sadness, crying for strength, and crying for understanding. This was one time I wanted to question God and ask where He was and why was He allowing it to happen.

"I'm sorry Daddy, for what I said earlier," Dynasty said, breaking the silence between us.

"You don't have to apologize, baby girl," I told her.

"Yes I do. It was an unfair statement and I just let the anger I felt take over. It was like if I could make myself believe what I said, the pain would go away," she said, as I wiped her round face that resembled her mother's so much.

Before any of us had a chance to say anything further, Cadence cried out, at the same time the doorbell rang. None of us were expecting anyone and it was almost eight at night, so I had no clue as to who it could be.

"You guys expecting anyone?" I asked just to make sure, but everyone shook their heads.

I took a few seconds to wipe my face and straighten out my clothes, before I headed downstairs to the door. Opening the door, I found Detective Ramos who was at the hospital the day of Veronica's accident. We hadn't seen him since we figured out what had really happened to cause Veronica to lose focus and get hit by the utility truck. Not only was he here, but so were Iesha's parents and a woman I didn't know.

"Uh, hello Detective, Mr. and Mrs. Ames; how are you? Is everything okay?" I asked even more worried than I had been previously.

"Is it okay if we come in, Pastor? I think there are some things that you need to hear," Mr. Ames spoke up.

"Please, call me Marcus and sure, come on in," I said, moving aside so that they could enter.

As I led them to the living room, MJ was coming down the stairs with Cadence wrapped tight in his arms, and Destiny and Dynasty right behind him.

"Well, we are sorry about just barging in here like this unannounced, but there is something that we need to let you all know," Detective Ramos started.

Before he could go any further, MJ entered and said, "Oh my God."

"Son, what's wrong?" I asked, and then followed his eyes to the elderly woman who had come in with everyone else.

Instead of him answering me he just stared at her before saying, "Grandma?"

Chapter *Seven*

Veronica

Look, I know what you are all thinking and quite honestly, I could care less right now. I have spent all of my young and adult years, doing and living for everyone else. It was now time that I live for Veronica. It's time that I start doing me. Especially after watching that video of the man that I thought I would be with forever, let another woman do things to him that were only made for our marriage bed.

No, I wasn't a saint and there are many things that I've done that I'm not proud of, but never during the whole time Marcus and I have been together have I stepped outside of our marriage. I guess my vows meant more than his. I did hate that I wasn't there with my kids and my new grandbaby, but sometimes you have to make a sacrifice for your own happiness. I was tired of people judging me and everything I did. Even if I wasn't doing anything wrong those, ole bourgeois bible thumpers always had something to say, no matter how nice and cordial I was. So since they wanted to talk, now they really had something to talk about.

I don't know what it was about this broad Adrian, but something wasn't right. Besides her looking familiar, I didn't know her from a can of paint, but she acted like she knew ya' girl or something. Every time I turned around, she was mugging me or saying something slick. She looked like she wanted to try it tonight in this club, but me on this liquid courage would set her straight. One of these Arabs was about to let her use one of those towels off their heads to wipe this trick's blood up in a minute, if she didn't get her life to capacity real fast.

Arms in the air, hips rolling, and butt poppin', I was turning this place out all by myself. Man, I haven't had this much carefree fun in so long I almost forgot what it felt like, but I guess I had Iesha to thank for that. The heifer may have been looney as all get out, but that didn't stop her from loving her some me.

Adrian thought I didn't see her get on her phone and exit the VIP, but I did. Iesha was too busy putting a show for some of these dudes, by rubbing all over her body and being all close to me, but I wasn't on that tonight. I just wanted to pour up, drink up, and throw a few stacks before the night was over.

All of a sudden my bladder starting twerking, and the bathroom was calling my name. I excused myself and hurried to the bathroom. I made it to the toilet just in time to let the waterfall flow. I was wiping myself and about to exit when I heard Adrian enter, talking on her phone. I thought, let me see what this strumpet got going on, as I sat back down and waited.

"No Patrick, I need it now!" I heard her say, and immediately my interest was piqued.

"Red eye, green eye, purple eye, I don't care what kind of ticket you get me. All I know is if I don't have it in the next thirty minutes, when I see you you're gonna have a black eye! Now get it done you incompetent bastard!" she said, trying to calm herself down before exiting the ladies room.

Where in the world was she going, and why didn't we know she was leaving? The plan was that Patrick was going to let us know when we could come back to the states so that we could enter undetected. I didn't want to go back to Atlanta and I shole' didn't want to go to Chicago. Adrian said she had some people out in Cali who owed her some favors, so that's where we were headed. But if she was leaving ahead of time, then you better believe something in the milk ain't clean.

Chapter *Eight*

Marcus

Grandma? What on earth was MJ talking about, I thought to myself, as the woman he was looking at had a lone tear rolling down her face.

"Yes baby, it's me. I'm your grandmother Sarita," the lady said.

Now I didn't know about anyone else, but I felt like the wind had been knocked out of me when she said her name. I always knew her name, but had never even seen her before.

Veronica didn't have not one picture of her in the house, so how did MJ know exactly who she was? Before I could ask what I was thinking, he stepped right on in and answered the question plaguing my mind.

"I know this may sound strange, but I had a dream about her the other night. God showed me her face and told me that she was coming. He didn't tell me why, He just told me to be prepared. I didn't say anything because so much had been going on, and a small part of me thought that maybe I was trippin'. That is, until she just walked through the door," he explained.

"Marcus, I found her," Mrs. Verna stepped in.

"Why?" I asked. I was so confused that nothing was making sense to me.

"Well after we finally left to go back home after the whole church thing, I got to thinking about why I felt so strong about Veronica when I first met her. I thought that maybe it was because God was just showing me what I needed in order to help her to repent and turn her life over to Him, but that wasn't just it. I knew she looked familiar and I just couldn't put my finger on it, until one day I was going through some old photos, just reminiscing on when times were good or what not, and I came across an old church retreat photo," Mrs. Verna explained. I was hoping this was going somewhere, because right now I just needed answers.

"In the photo was a woman who was about four months pregnant and had a daughter who was around seven or eight at the time. Looking at that picture, everything came back to me like it had happened yesterday.

We had just had an opening word from our Bishop before the church retreat festivities were to begin. There were games, food, music, just some good ole fellowship. You could always tell when someone was new was visiting our church,

because they stuck out like a sore thumb.

I had watched this young lady walk over to one of the tables, with her daughter clinging closely to her side. Everyone seemed to be in their own little worlds instead of welcoming one of God's children like they should have. That's one of the reasons that people didn't like going to church, I thought to myself. People can tell when they are welcomed or not, and if you are trying to bring the people of God to Him, they have to see Him through what's inside of you. I guess some people just think it's too hard to give a genuine smile or hug.

The young lady was dressed very well, and her daughter was one of the most beautiful little girls I had ever seen outside of my own. Her beautiful brown eyes held so many questions, and I knew it would be a long time before she got any of the answers.

I told Bernard that I would be right back so that I could go and give her a warm welcome.

"Well praise the Lord. Aren't you just a beautiful little lady," I said to the little girl, as she smiled up at me with her two front teeth missing.

"Thank you. My name is Veronica," she replied. She had such good manners.

"It's nice to meet you, Veronica. I'm Mrs. Ames," I said smiling down at her, before turning my attention to her mother.

"It's nice to meet you Mrs. Ames, I'm Sarita. You were the only one who came over to greet us and I thank you for that. I was about to leave because it felt so unwelcoming," she said.

"Oh baby, I know how that can be. But always remember God will never lead you anywhere to be alone. We just have to be open enough to receive the people that He sends our way. So do you live around here?" I asked, seeing the liquid sadness fill her eyes.

"Little Miss Veronica, do you want to go play with the other kids?" I asked, so that I could talk with Sarita alone. Before I could say more, she was running off to the other children. That's when the dam broke and the water started flowing freely.

"Come sweetie," I said, as I helped her over to one of the unoccupied benches and sat beside her. I handed her a napkin from off of the table, and allowed her to get it all out before I began speaking again.

"I know that you don't know me, and whatever it is seems to be heavy on your heart and mind, but I am a good listening ear; even if my husband thinks I talk more than I listen," I chuckled, trying to lighten the mood.

"I don't know where to begin," she said with her head hung low.

"Well for starters, you can lift up your head. I don't care what is going on in your life; you always hold your head up high. Walk around with the boldness of God permeating through you. Do you hear what I'm saying to you dear?"

"Yes ma'am," she said, as she sat up straight and looked me in my eyes.

"Now that's better," I said, waiting on her to begin.

"Well, as you can see I'm pregnant. I just found out and I'm terrified to tell my husband."

"Why is that?" I asked. I knew this was about to be some mess, and I prayed ahead of time God gave me the right words to say.

"He doesn't want another baby and I know that he will continue to make me do things that I don't want to," she said, beginning to cry and drop her head again.

"Unt uh, hold that head up," I said, using my pointer finger to lift her chin up. "What will he make you do?"

"He will make me sell my body. He wanted our first daughter and he treats her like the little princess she is, but he told me from the time I had her that if I was to ever get pregnant again, he would trick me out until I either miscarried or he will kill me himself. I can't take that chance with this baby."

"My God. Do you have any family here or somewhere that you and your daughter can go?"

"No ma'am. He knows all of the family that I have and where to find me if I go there."

"What if I can talk with our Bishop and see if we can provide a safe place for you and your daughter to be?"

"Oh No! I can't take Veronica from her father! He would surely kill me then. I have to leave her with him if I leave," she said now full of panic.

"What do you mean? You can't leave her with him if he is as bad as you say that he is." This girl was talking crazy right about now. There was no way she could leave her child like that.

"At least if I leave her here, he will be focused on taking care of her and not worry about looking for me. Maybe he would think I was dead altogether and I can have this baby safely. I know he would never hurt Veronica. He loves her more than he loves me, and I'm his wife," she finished and wiped her face dry.

I just sat there looking at her, not knowing what to say next, when Veronica ran back over to us.

"Mommy, come on, they are doing face painting and I want us to have matching faces," she said, with her eyes full of innocence.

"Okay baby, here I come. Let me just tell Mrs. Ames goodbye and then we can have our faces painted. We are going to have to leave soon and get home, so daddy won't miss us."

"Okay mommy. Bye Mrs. Ames, I'll see you later," she said, running off towards the face painting station.

"Thank you for at least listening to me. Let your husband know that you are an awesome listener," she laughed, as she started to walk off.

"Wait," I said stopping her in her tracks. "Take my number and address so if you ever need anything, you can call me or come by." I wrote down my information and handed her the piece of paper.

I watched her walk off towards the table and sit down as the photographer took her and her daughter's photo.

"Once the event was over, I asked the Deacon Willis if I could have that picture that he had taken of Sarita and her daughter, because I wanted to send it to her. I didn't realize that I had only given her my info and I had none of hers in order to send it," Mrs. Verna explained.

"Verna prayed day and night over that one picture. She prayed that God would cover, comfort and protect them. She asked that no matter what Sarita decided to do, that they would have their chance to be together again as a family," Mr. Ames joined in.

"And the day that Iesha brought Veronica home to meet us I knew that it was her. She had the same beautiful eyes even though the innocence was long gone. I wanted so badly to ask where her mother and sibling were, but for some reason God wouldn't allow me to utter a word. No matter how strongly we feel about certain things, we have to listen to God if He advises us to keep quiet. How does that saying go? Uh, loose lips sink ships or something like that. We have to know when to speak and when to just keep quiet and pray," she told everyone in that room. It wasn't time for a sermon, but we all needed to hear this. Silence is not a sign of weakness but one of strength. It takes a very strong person to be able to be quiet in the times of adversity, and just fall on your knees and

pray.

Chapter *Nine*

Iesha

The turn up was too real tonight! These Arabs knew how to get it in. They had the bottle service going, the music blasting, and the big faces falling. I wasn't a stripper, but I made some stacks tonight just doing me.

Veronica told me once she came back from the bathroom, that she needed to tell me something once we got back to the hotel, but I wasn't trying to have a serious conversation now or later. I just wanted to get my freak on, and I noticed one of the sexiest men in the room had been constantly watching us. Why not give him a show?

I laced Veronica's drink with a few crushed up ecstasy pills and waited for the alcohol and drugs to take effect. It didn't take long either. Before I knew it, she was all over lil daddy, and he was loving it. You could see the smile forming on his face, even with his long thick beard that was shaped up nicely. His skin and his eyes were the color of coffee that had a splash of creamer in it, and he stood about six feet two. I always thought that these men were short, or maybe it was just that big towel he had on his head that gave him an extra few inches. Speaking of inches...never mind, here I go again with these impure thoughts of mine. But I was definitely gonna find out about those inches later, and I wasn't talking about bundles of hair either.

The club was about to close for the night and we had been on lil daddy heavy for the night, when I finally realized that Adrian was nowhere to be found. After she walked off earlier on her phone, I didn't think much of her disappearance until just this moment. All of the drinks, money and men had me forgetting all about her.

"Ron, have you seen Adrian?" I asked. Veronica was drunk as a skunk and could barely stand up. I don't even know why I asked her because right about now, she probably didn't even know her own name.

"She's gone," Veronica said, barely able to stand up. Ole boy that she was with had to help her to her feet, just as an idea hit me. An evil smirk came across my face as I asked him, "Why don't you come back to our room for a little after party?"

Licking his lips while looking from me to Veronica with that sexy smile, he began to light up the room.

"Give me a minute," he said in that thick accent of his, as he walked over to who I assumed was his crew. I watched him as he said something to them and they all looked over in our direction. They all looked like money and I bet if I was near them, they would smell like it too.

After a few more moments, he walked back over to us with two of his friends. I could tell he was definitely the baller and sexiest of them all just, by the way his presence demanded everyone's undivided attention.

"You gorgeous ladies mind if my two friends come along?" he asked.

"The more the merrier," Veronica said, leaning up against him as he smiled at her. I knew he was thinking the same thing that I was, but he didn't know why I was thinking the same thing. They would all find out soon enough.

I knew why Veronica used to pimp me out extra hard, beat me, and even verbally abuse me. She found out that I was behind the set up of her father being murdered, but she didn't know that I was on to her. I loved her so much that I never even said anything to her about it. But now after all of these years, I was able to give her a dose of her own medicine with help from these three gentlemen. Don't trip! God knew I was going to do it even before I did, so I knew this was one of the times that the Almighty was letting me have

my way. Ain't God good?

Chapter *Ten*

Iesha

It was almost three in the afternoon by the time I got up the next day. Last night was epic, as I lay there thinking about the movie we had just made. Well the one I made, because Veronica didn't even know she was on camera. This would be my little secret for now, or so I thought.

"You think because I became saved and a preacher's wife that I lost all my street smarts, huh?" Veronica asked me, as she sat in the corner watching me and blowing smoke from her mouth into the air. Since being in Dubai, we got hooked on that good good. I don't know what they put in it, but we needed this back in the states. Smoking would never be the same once we returned.

Coming back from my thoughts, I asked nonchalantly, "What are you talking about bae?"

"Bae? Humph. Seems like you forgot who I be," she said, now getting up and walking over to the bed and pushing me back down before I could get up all the way. This couldn't have been good. I remembered the look in her eyes too well, and although I was bout that life, this look always terrified me. It was that look of "shoot first and ask questions never" like that book I read by some lady named Star, Sky, nah, that wasn't it. What was her name? Oh I remember, Fanita Moon Pendleton, that was her name. When I had a lot of time on my hands, I was all into her books. At the moment I felt like I was in one of them right now, and the way Veronica was looking at me was like she was about to off me.

"What are you talking about Veronica? Move so I can go to the bathroom. I gotta pee," I said, trying to move around her. She was using all of her weight to keep me in place though.

"Just remember I will always be that HBIC, even when you think I'm not. You wanted me back so you better be ready to handle it," she said, as she backed away towards the dresser.

Turning her back and then facing me again, I was hit in the face with a stack of money and a folded up piece of paper.

"If you were really bout that life, you would have known you can't beat a bawss at a game that I created. Since when have you ever seen me leave a drink unattended anywhere then come back to it? I knew you would call yourself trying to outshine me, but baby, didn't I teach you that you would always be ten steps behind me?

I was so surprised to see my boy Barakah and his twin brother's Fadil and Farid last night, and it was just like old times. They had been taught the game by their father Hassan just like my dad taught me. How do you think I knew about all the hot spots to go to since we been here? My dad would fly us out here at least once a year to hang with Hassan. At one time I had a thing for Barakah, with his fine self. Thanks to you, I finally got me a piece of him last night. I guess you are good for something," she said smiling, while I looked on in shock.

"Close your mouth honey, that's not flattering. You should never open your mouth that wide if the reason you're doing it doesn't bring me any dead presidents back, if you know what I mean."

That little joke had her falling out laughing, but I saw nothing funny. All I could see was red. Once again, I let my feelings for Veronica get in the way and I missed being played, yet again by her.

"But-" I started just to be cut off by her.

"No sweetie, you have been talking too much. Now it's my time. Your mouth always seems to get you in trouble. If you kept your mouth shut sometimes, then little Miss Adrian wouldn't be running her mouth right now," she said really confusing me.

"Learn to shut up sometimes and maybe you can keep your hoes in check so they wouldn't have a chance to turn on you," she finished, as she walked into the bathroom and turned on the shower.

I had no clue what she was talking about, as I unfolded the piece of paper and noticed Adrian's handwriting.

Iesha,

Let me start off by saying that you know I love you, but I can't do this with you anymore. After all I've lost and everything I've done to be with you, it still doesn't feel worth it. I know there is a part of you that is scared of the outcome of it all, but I'm not willing to risk anymore than I already have. This decision I'm making will indeed cost me my freedom, but I'm woman enough now to take that. As cliché as it may sound, finding God was the answer and it caused me to see myself and my situation for what it really was. If I could take it all back I would, but we know life doesn't work that way.

Please don't look at this as me turning on you, but as me trying to help. You need help, Iesha, and after the phone call I made a week ago, I know it was for the best. I really care about you and this is by far harder than anything that I have ever done before.

I've been wrong all of this time about my sister. Veronica had nothing to do with what I went through without her or our father, Clarence in my life. She didn't even know about me. All of these years I was thinking that she knew about me and wanted nothing to do with me, but I couldn't have been further from the truth. And when I met you and found out who you were to her, it was like you confirmed everything I thought I knew. I was so pressed to make her pay for the suffering my mother and I went through.

It was your mother who finally told me the truth, and God knows I wish I had known all of this time. I would have been with my sister, my family, and she wouldn't have had to go on all of these years not knowing where our mother was. She thought she had abandoned her or worse, died, Iesha! Don't you get how messed up that was for her? But no, your sick and twisted mind made you think it was all good. That's okay though. I'm going to fix this with the help of our mothers and God. I pray that both He and Veronica and everyone else that my actions hurt, forgives me for my involvement in this.

Trust and believe, when I find out where Keith took my sister, I'll do everything in my power to bring her back to her family; the ones who really love her, no matter what she has gone through in life; the ones who are worried to death, because they don't know where she is or even if she's okay.

It makes me sick to my stomach to know I played a part in hurting them, and if God will allow me, I will make it up to them one way or another. I'm praying for you too, Iesha, and I hope one day you can find some peace.

I know being locked up in that hospital day in and day out is taking you away from reality. That's why I'm writing you, hoping this will bring you back in order to get the help you really need and deserve, so that you can function in life normally. Your mother explained to me, how you sit in your room and have conversations with Veronica, even me, and we are not even there. Look around you Iesha, and don't be afraid to ask for the help that you need. Maybe one day you can really get to visit Dubai, because I know that has been one of your dreams for as long as I've known you. Get yourself better so that you can go. No matter what I will always love you.

Adrian

"What in the world was she talking about? I wasn't in a mental hospital. She was the one that sounded crazy right about now," I said, throwing the letter on the floor.

"VERONICA! VERONICA! GET IN HERE NOW YOU GOOD FOR NOTHING STRUMPET! YOU THINK I DON'T KNOW YOU ARE PLAYING WITH ME?! I TOLD YOU NOT TO PLAY WITH ME EVER AGAIN IN LIFE ,BUT I SEE YOU DON'T LISTEN! GET IN HERE VERONICA!" I yelled at the top of my lungs, as I heard the bathroom door open.

"That's what I thought!" I said, as I turned around to see two big men in white uniforms and that doctor lady that I didn't like, standing there looking at me.

"Iesha, you know that Veronica is not here. Let's go to my office so we can talk," she said walking towards me.

"Don't you come near me! Where is Veronica?" I yelled, as I pulled on my hair.

"Well that's what I was hoping that you would tell us. Did Keith hurt her? Where is she, Iesha? Does she need help?" she asked me as she walked closer to me.

"She doesn't need help but you are about to!" I said lunging toward her. I was so focused on getting my hands around her neck, that I hadn't noticed the two orderlies coming up on each side of me, until it was too late. The last thing I remembered was Dr. Flannigan sticking that syringe full of a sedative in my arm, before everything went black.

Chapter *Eleven*

Keith

I don't know how I ended up in this mess that I was now in. I had my whole life ahead of me with a career to match, and I was about to lose it. Not about to, I'm sure I had already lost it and all behind a woman. My mama always told me that I should take the time to know who I was in God, so when he presented me with my wife I would know right away.

My dad was never one to beat you over the head with scripture, so he just gave it to me real. He always kept it simple when he told me, "Son, never trust a big butt and a smile." I always laughed it off thinking he was just quoting that old school song by Bell, Biv, Devoe, but looks like they all were right. Adrian was straight poison. All pun intended.

I'll never forget the day I was called into my boss's office at work and saw this gorgeous woman sitting before me. When she turned around to look at me, I knew that she had heard and felt me suck all of the air out of the room.

She had me stuck like chuck.

Now that I think back on everything, I see how God tried to warn me, but I didn't take heed to it. I know I'm not the only one that has heard or seen a warning from God that was as clear as day, but instead of doing what it is we know is right, we put those blinders on and end up crashing into a brick wall because of it.

I would give anything in order to change it, but that initial conversation we had the day we met changed everything.

*****

"Williams, this is your new partner, Officer Adrian Norman," Lt. Frazier said to me like it was a done deal, and not up for discussion. He didn't

have to worry about that, because I had no problems taking this order.

"Nice to meet you, Officer," she said in a seductive voice, that made me immediately adjust my uniform pants.

"Same here. Welcome to the force," I said, clearing my throat and reaching my hand out to shake hers. Man, her hand was smooth like silk and I wondered if the rest of her body was as well.

"Thanks. So you ready to head out and clean up the city?" she asked me, with that killer smile that instantly lit up the room and my heart. Something about this woman was magnetic, and I

should have listened to the voice that was going off in my head warning me, but I didn't.

"After you officer," I said, opening the door so that she could go out before me.

Before walking out of the office, she winked at me and as she slowly passed, I saw a bubble so sweet that Bubblicious Bubble Gum couldn't have the recipe for. This flavor was one of a kind and I guess my face showed my exact thoughts.

"Son, off the record, be careful with that one. Keep it strictly professional. Something tells me that if you don't, I won't be able to get you out of that mess," my lieutenant said to me, bringing me out of my daydream.

I looked at him with a smirk on my face and said, "Well, you know will always present the woman to the man when it's time."

"Keith, everything that is placed before you is not always God. Always remember that the devil knows God's word too, and will put things in front of us that we think are from God, and it will cause us more heartache than we could have ever imagined. That's why a true relationship with Him is needed so we can know the difference when we are faced with different situations. I don't want to talk your head off, but just be careful," he schooled me.

"Yes sir," I said, walking out and heading to the front door to meet up with my new partner. I should have taken that little tidbit of wisdom with me, but I left it right in that office with my superior.

"So how do you like the area so far?" I asked Adrian to try and break the ice.

"It's nice. I've been here plenty of times and fell in love with it. That's why when the position came open, I jumped on it the first chance that I got," She replied.

There was something about the way that she said "jumped on it", and how she was looking at me with this sexy smirk on her face, that had me feeling some kind of way.

"Ahem. Well this is home for me. I was born in Macon, GA, and when I was five, my mom and dad moved me and my two sisters to Atlanta, and we have been here ever since," I said, giving a little background on myself.

"That's nice. Typical American family, huh? Did you have a little white picket fence and a dog named Spot too?" she said with a different attitude and anger lacing her voice.

Before I had a chance to respond, she apologized.

"Hey, I'm sorry Williams. It's just that I was raised alone by my mother while my father and sister lived it up. To this day, I blame them both for the suffering and struggling, my mother and I had to endure. But I was wrong to take it out on you. I just wished I had that growing up that's all. Now, enough about all of that. I saw how you were watching me back there. You trying to swim in my love pool?" she asked, before falling out laughing and causing me to join in. This was going to be an interesting partnership.

Chapter *Twelve*

Keith

As time went on, we got closer and closer. We even started going to church together. I had heard about Clover Hill Church of God in Christ, from a few of my coworkers who attended on the regular, but had never thought about going until Adrian suggested we go. She said that she felt us getting closer and understood that we were partners at work, but she wanted to be partners outside of work.

I had never met a woman in my life that was so direct and straight forward like her, and it was one of the most attractive things I had ever seen. Since my feelings were growing as well, we both decided to take it slow and keep it hidden from everyone for the time being.

If I hadn't been so blind to what was really going on around me, then I would have clearly understood the message that was given on my very first visit to the church.

I will admit though, as soon as you stepped into the church, you could definitely feel the presence of God. There was no denying that at all, but my mind was wandering off every chance it got. I had seen Adrian on plenty occasions in regular street clothes, but today she had me stuck on stupid. Her long hair was cascading down her back, stopping right before it hit her behind, and her medium brown face with the beauty mark under her right eye, held just the right amount of makeup to bring out all of that beauty. She had on a navy blue pantsuit that left nothing to the imagination, a red silk blouse under the jacket, and some red pumps that I wouldn't mind seeing her wear again. She could lose the clothes though.

Praise and worship was so good it had the whole church on their feet, giving God glory just for who He is. Even I had to give a couple of thanks because if it wasn't for Him, I could have lost my life a long time ago being a police officer. So He could definitely get some thanks from me. Things were going good, but something in the atmosphere shifted once the Pastor got up to speak, and caused Adrian to get noticeably uncomfortable.

"Good morning people of God," Pastor Millhouse started. I was surprised to see such a young man like him leading such a big church like this. But I guess when God calls you, age doesn't matter.

"Morning Pastor," the church responded, all but Adrian.

"Before I get started, I want to just honor God for waking us all up in our right minds this morning. It's because of Him we can come and fellowship today," he said in his opening.

"Yes it is!" one of the mothers and a few of the other members said out loud.

"To my beautiful wife Veronica and our children, don't they look wonderful this morning?" he said beaming with pride, as I looked over in the direction he was looking.

First Lady Millhouse looked radiant in her coral jumpsuit, with a teal colored blazer and strappy teal sandals to match. Her face held simply some lip gloss, but she was one of the most beautiful women I had ever seen in my life.

Her long hair was full of bouncy curls and her

smiled outshined the sun. I understood why

Pastor married her, she was definitely a banger!

But there was also something about her that was

very familiar to me that I just couldn't put my

finger on. I didn't have long to try and jog my

memory, before I was pulled out of my thoughts

by the sound of the church saying, "Amen" and

lifting up their heads. I guess there was a prayer I

missed. My fault God.

"Family, I had a different message prepared

today but as I was sitting in my office before God

this morning, He spoke to me about something

totally different. So forgive me if I don't have all of my notes for this, but I know God will get this word across to you all.

How many of you know what an anagram is?" he paused to see if he would get any answers, and when there was none, he continued.

"An anagram is a type of wordplay that when you rearrange the letters of words or phrases a certain way, a new word or phrase is created. Let me give you a few examples so you can understand before I move on.

If you take this one 'the eyes' and rearrange the letters using all letters once, you now have 'they see'. A few more examples, 'conversation' changes to 'voices rant on', 'Eleven plus two' is now 'twelve plus one', and my all time favorite, 'mother-in-law' turns to 'Woman Hitler'," he said laughing at the last one.

When I sat there thinking about it, I had to laugh myself because I had never thought about anything like that, but it all made sense. I could look around and see that so many other people were shocked as well.

"We ourselves can a lot of times be an anagram. Some of us do it unconsciously and some of us do it knowingly. How many times have we put up a front to have people thinking one way about us, but in all reality we are totally opposite of what we portray?" he asked.

Only a few hands went up as he waited briefly again. It stunned me that not only did those few people admit that they put on a front by raising their hands, but he and First Lady raised theirs as well.

"I raise my hand because I myself at one time was one of those pretenders, but once I fully committed to God, I had to change the way that I was from the inside out.

I understand that we make it seem like we have it all together and can dress up the outside, but the inside is still messed up. But you better *believe you can only do that so long before God will reveal you to yourself, and if you don't take heed then He will reveal you to others.*

Not only that, we should be very careful of the company we keep. If we aren't able to discern the spirit in others that is not of God they can cause much greater harm to us than we could have ever imagined.

We have two spirits that we deal with. The first being the spirit of God and the other, of course, is the spirit of the antichrist. Because we live in this world that accepts the spirit of the antichrist more than the spirit of our heavenly

Father, it's so much harder to know who is who if you don't have that connection with God.

You can be in cahoots with the devil and not even realize it. That's that wolf in sheep's clothing that is talked about in Matthew, chapter seven, verse fifteen where it says, 'Jesus warned us, watch out for false prophets. They come to you in sheep's clothing, but inwardly they are ferocious wolves.'

And don't think of just the false prophets in the church. People in our everyday lives can be those wolves disguising themselves. The very person that you are sitting next to can very well be that wolf dressed up in True Religion. No pun intended, and I hope no one in here is dressed in that name brand," he chuckled, while everyone was looking around the room. That's when I noticed Adrian wasn't beside me anymore. I brushed it off as her going to the bathroom and continued to listen. There was something tugging away at me but I threw it to the back of my mind.

"What I mean, is although they are wolves, you better believe that they, too, are discerning who has the spirit of God and who doesn't. They can smell their prey from miles away, and know that if your relationship with God is not a strong one and there is any way that they can get inside your head and heart, they will do it.

The bible says in first Peter, five and eight, 'Keep your mind clear, and be alert. Your opponent the devil is prowling around like a roaring lion as he looks for someone to devour.'

So here comes this anagram that you are thinking means one thing by showing you what you want to see, but in the end God will shift that thing around for you to see it as something totally different. By then it's too late, and we are so far in what we think that there is no way out.

Quite frankly, that's what they want us to think. They want us thinking that we are so far in that there is no way of escape, and that God has turned His back on us. I urge you today that if you are feeling that something in your life isn't right and you are wanting to get closer to God so that you an be able to effectively from this point forward be able to discern who the anagrams are before they switch it up on you, meet me down at the altar," he said, as he moved from behind his pulpit and walked to the bottom of the stairs.

Slowly but surely, people were getting up, walking towards him, and the tugging became stronger. Just as I was about to get up and make my way down there, I felt the presence of Adrian once again.

"Hey, I feel a little dizzy. Do you think we can go ahead and head out? Maybe getting some fresh air will help me," she said as she rubbed my forearm. Instantly I forgot what it was I was about to do, and got up to walk her out. I even held up the international church "excuse my departure" signal, of holding up my index finger while exiting.

"Why you do that?" Adrian asked me laughing.

"Do what?" I was confused.

"Hold your finger up?"

"I don't know. It was just something that I was taught growing up in church with my *parents." Up until this moment, I had never even asked why we did that in churches.*

"It comes from when the slaves when they were in church services and needed to be excused for the restroom or something. Since they weren't free, they had to ask permission for everything they did, and that finger you just put up signifies the ignorance we still have today. I guarantee Pastor does not mind if you get up to leave. Holding that finger up is more of a distraction than anything," she said, schooling me before getting in the car.

As I closed her door and walked over to get in the driver's seat, what she said made a lot of sense to me, I thought, as I started the car and backed out.

"You want to go back to my place for Sunday dinner?" she asked me.

This wasn't the first time I had been to her place and since she wasn't feeling good, I wanted to make sure she was straight before I headed home. Having a home cooked meal and being in her presence a little while longer was just what the doctor ordered for me, though.

We made small talk for the next twenty minutes as we drove to her apartment. It looked like she was feeling better and better the further away we got from the church. Right as we were pulling up to her apartment complex, my phone rung and my father's face popped up on the screen.

"What's good Pops?" I asked him, while pulling into a parking spot and getting out.

"Hey son what's going on?"

"Nothing much, just left church and about to have Sunday dinner with my partner before heading home. Everything good on your end?" I asked him.

"Your mother had a slight headache today so we didn't make our morning service. Instead we streamed in to hear Pastor Millhouse speak," he said.

"Oh yeah? That's where Adrian and I just left from. Service was on point but we had to leave a little early because she wasn't feeling too well either," I said excitedly, as I opened Adrian's door and helped her out. Her body had me stuck, as she brushed the front of her body up against mine causing me to tune everything out that my father was saying.

"Um Pops, let me call you back. I'll be over later after I eat and make sure she is okay. Tell Mom I said I love her and I'll see her in a few." I hung up without even waiting on a response from him.

"No you won't," Adrian said confusing me.

"Whatchu mean?" I asked as she unlocked her door and entered her apartment.

Without responding, she went over to the stereo system and I made my way over to the couch. Her apartment wasn't too big and it wasn't too small. It was just right for a single woman. Her living room was decorated in purple, silver, and black, with one of the most comfortable leather sectionals I had ever sat on. Her black entertainment center held her sixty-inch smart TV, along with surround sound speakers *throughout the room. She had her stereo and Xbox One connected to the system, and all of her games and movies lined up in the cabinet.*

Getting the remote off of the coffee table after removing her jacket, she turned her back to me and I noticed her shirt was backless. She had this tattoo going down the middle of her back that said something that I couldn't make out, but it was the sexiest thing I had ever seen on a woman.

"What's that say on your back?" I asked, as she turned on the system and August Alsina's "Porn Star" began playing. Without a word, she turned, kicked off her shoes, and walked over to

me never breaking the eye contact we had with each other.

' She ride it like she never gonna ride this again

She thinking like a G and she ain't never giving in

She ride it in the back of my car, on the bar,

On the stash, on the bed she ain't scared

'Cause when I lay back, shawty don't know how to act

She ready when the lights go off she climb on top

Her body rocking we don't stop

No handle bars or falling off, cause cause

She ride me like a porn star......'

I was speechless as I watched her move her body slow to the beat, and wondered if in her past life she was a stripper, because I'm sure those ladies down at Onyx could learn a thing or two from her.

Once again, she turned her back to me as she removed her shirt and sat backwards on my lap. I could now clearly see what the tat going down her spine read.

'Good girls go to heaven. Bad girls go everywhere else.'

I needed God to get down off of His throne this very second and come to my rescue, because if He didn't August was about to send us into another world, and there was no coming back from what we were about to do.

She sat back in my lap while continuing to rock her hips, and I almost lost it. I tried to speak and heard the words clearly in my head but my lips weren't moving. As soon as the song ended and the next began to play, she didn't break her stride. Getting up, she reached for my hand so that I could follow her into her bedroom.

"Wait. Are you sure that you want to do this?" I asked her. I should have been asking myself that question instead.

She stopped walking and moved closer to me, and without a word planted her lips on mine. Our tongues spoke a language that at the time wasn't heavenly like it should have been, but more worldly than anything known to man. As she pulled away from me and I looked into her eyes, I knew that she was telling me that all things were a go.

*****

That first time with Adrian took me down a road with no end, as I think about what I was doing right now. Sex with just anyone can definitely turn your world upside down, I realized as I sat here thinking. Before I could think any further, I heard the sound that I had become all too familiar with over the last few months.

I got up from the couch in the living room and headed to the kitchen to get some cleaning supplies and a ginger ale, before going into the guest bedroom. Opening the door and seeing the sight before me continued to break my heart, but not enough for me to divert away from the original plan that was put in place.

By now, the need for me to be with Adrian, far away on an island having sex on a private beach, with millions of dollars in an off shore account, meant more to me than what was going on in this house. If I failed what we had started at, she would never forgive me; so this is just the way it had to be until I got word on our next move. With Iesha locked away, it was all me and Adrian from here on out.

For a split second, I felt bad looking at Veronica in this position she was in. She knew she had probably been taken, per Iesha's request, but had no idea that it was her long lost sister who hated everything about her, and was in on the plan.

Veronica was weary and probably had given up on everything and everyone she thought would come and help her. No one knew where we were. Adrian wanted me to take Veronica somewhere that no one would even think of looking for us. Orders were to stay put, until she called me to tell me what to do next.

"Please Keith, I can't take this anymore. I think something is wrong," Veronica said, sounding weaker by the day.

"You know I can't do that. Here, drink your ginger ale and eat these crackers. They will settle your stomach some," I said, handing her the drink before I started to sanitize the room.

"It's been almost seven months now," she said with tears in her eyes.

I said nothing, as I tried my best to ignore her and her pleas in order to clean up and get out of there, before she started praying again. It seemed like each time I came in here, she would hold me long enough to break out in prayer. I guess she hoped the prayers would change my mind, but they never did.

I was trying my best to hurry along, and right before I walked out of the room, Veronica said something that made my heart stop.

"Keith, I think my water just broke."

Chapter *Thirteen*

Marcus

"She's pregnant?! My daughter is pregnant?" Sarita said, jumping up as it was just revealed to everyone, including me, that Veronica was indeed pregnant. We had suspicions right before everything had gone down at the church, but nothing had been confirmed. Veronica wanted to tell the kids when we went on vacation if it was true, but since that never happened, it had been placed in the back of my mind until now.

I had informed the detectives and police that were on her case, so they would be aware. That's why they were doing all that they could in order to get her back. They told me not to even mention it to anyone else, because they didn't want us to worry any more than we were. I don't think I could have been worried any more than I already was. That information wasn't made public because they didn't want Veronica to be hurt any further. I felt that it may have given her kidnappers an ounce of sympathy towards her if they knew she was with child.

I don't even know what we are having since that would have made her only a little over a month along when she was taken. I had no clue if she and the baby were okay, or if she had been hurt or so stressed so bad, that the baby didn't make it. I was worried sick with the unknown.

"Mom was having another baby?" Destiny asked me, with a sad smile on her face.

"I guess she was baby girl. She couldn't have been that far along and because her tubes were tied, we never thought she would have more kids. I guess we would have found out on her last follow-up appointment, right before we left on the vacation," I said, thinking back over everything that had and hadn't happened.

"I wonder if it's a boy or a girl. Or maybe another set of twins!" Dynasty said getting excited, and causing my head to pop up. I hadn't even thought about having one more child let alone another set of twins.

"Well, as long as the baby is healthy and we get your mother back safe and sound, I don't care what it is we are having," I said honestly.

"I'm excited and all about the baby, but that is a little ratchet. I mean, mom is pregnant at the same time her future daughter-in-law was pregnant. Cadence isn't even a month old yet," Destiny said, causing everyone in the room to laugh a little.

"Don't call our mother ratchet," MJ defended his mom. Although we were all worried, it was good to see the smiles on my babies' faces.

We were all so focused on the information that Detective Ramos had just given us that we didn't notice Mr. Ames had left the room, until he was coming back in as he was getting off of his phone.

"Excuse me, I have to take this call," Detective Ramos spoke up, as he walked out.

"Sure, take your time Detective," I said, as I looked back into the face of Iesha's father. It was crazy how this one woman was hurting so many people, and didn't even seem to care about her own family.

Mr. Bernard and Mrs. Verna were the sweetest people you would ever want to meet, and to know how much they loved their daughter and to see them hurting behind her all at the same time, made me sick to my stomach. They reminded me so much of my parents who had passed away years ago. I'd give anything to have them in our lives again. Their daughter may have been wrecking my home and life, but her parents were a blessing to us just by being concerned.

"That was the hospital," Mr. Ames said as he rubbed the back of his head and took a deep breath.

"Nard, what's wrong?" Mrs. Verna asked calling him by his nickname.

"Dr. Flannigan called and said they had to put Iesha back in solitary and sedate her," he wearily said, as he sat back beside her.

"Why, what happened?" Sarita asked.

"Apparently for the last week or two, they had been watching Iesha on the camera that they have in her room. You know they monitor her just to make sure that she doesn't try to harm herself. Well, while they have been watching her, they figured out that she had removed herself from reality and was living out what she wanted to be happening. Dr. Flannigan said it's an illness called Delusional Disorder, where the person can't tell what is real from what is imagined," he explained.

"Finally a name for it," Mrs. Verna said. "Iesha has always talked to herself and made up these elaborate scenarios that no one could tell her was not really happening. She really believed everything she thought was going on around her."

"She had gotten medicines that were to help her over the years, but no one really knew the name of what she was fighting, until Dr. Flannigan started seeing her after she got arrested for the church incident.

The doctor said that Iesha thought she was in Dubai with both Veronica and Adrian. They were supposedly on this luxurious getaway, waiting on a call from that crooked Detective Johansen to let them know when it was okay to come back to the states. I guess she didn't want to acknowledge that she killed him inside the church that day.

Anyway, from the conversations she had with herself, she thought that Adrian was jealous of Veronica and wanted to have Iesha all to herself. Dr. Flannigan said she would change her voice to sound like each person and everything. This was the reality that she wanted to happen," he finished.

"Well, what happened for them to have to sedate and confine her if she was only talking to herself?" I asked.

"It was a letter from Adrian. In the letter she explained that she was sorry for her involvement and that she had made a call a week ago. It was asking her to please let us know where Keith had taken Veronica so that she could come back to her family; when she got to the end of the letter, she spazzed out. Thinking she could calm Iesha down, Dr. Flannigan calmly went to her asking if she wanted to sit down and discuss what was going on, and that's when she lunged at her. They had to sedate her for her safety as well as theirs. When she came to again, she was a lot calmer. The meds made her think clearly, and that's when she told them Keith had her, but she didn't give any more information. She shut down," Mr. Ames said.

"Keith? You mean the one she was engaged to?" I asked shocked?

"Adrian was engaged?" asked her mother Sarita.

"Yea. On the first day of our counseling session is when she filmed us; the one Iesha showed in church," I said, standing up and pacing the floor. I couldn't believe that I let that feeling I had in the pit of my stomach about them, get pushed to the back of my mind. Now it all made sense that it was a setup.

"We have to go out and find this Keith then," Mrs. Verna said.

"No need," Detective Ramos said coming back into the room.

"Why not?" I asked. "He could know where my wife is!" I said starting to get angry. There was no way that I could be held accountable for whatever I did, if my wife and unborn child weren't brought home unharmed.

"That call that I just took was my superior telling me that we had our IT guys trying to get a signal on Officer Williams' phone."

"OFFICER!" everyone in the room yelled. We had no idea that Keith was a police officer.

"Yes, he's one of our officers. He's been on the force for almost fifteen years now. Our Lieutenant thought they would be a good team, but right before everything happened, he felt he needed to assign Officer Norman somewhere else."

"What's taking them so long to find them then if he has a police issued phone with GPS?" MJ asked. He had been pretty quiet, but I could see he was almost to his breaking point too.

"Officer Williams is very intelligent and good at what he does. We never had reason to check up on his whereabouts until all of this took place. It was at that time when we found out that his phone had been tampered with, so the signal isn't able to be traced at this time. It's gonna take some time, but we will get a location soon," Detective Ramos said about to leave and head back to the station.

"Detective, before you go, I would like for all of us to pray," Sarita said and everyone agreed.

"Sure. God's word does say where two or three have come together in my name, I am there among them," Detective responded, as we all stood around the room and held hands.

"Mrs. Verna, will you lead us in prayer?" Sarita asked.

She squeezed her hand and gave her a warm smile while shaking her head. "No baby. God hears you too. Go before Him on behalf of your daughters and your family. You have all of our support."

I watched as Destiny and Dynasty got on each side of Sarita, and MJ stood behind them with his arms stretched around them all. I moved from my position on the other side of Mrs. Verna so that I could go and cover my children and mother-in-law. I was still the head of this family, and I wouldn't feel right if I didn't stand beside them right now.

"Lord, I know that I don't come to you as often as I should, and for that I'm sorry. I understand now that I have to be closer to you in order to be the best mother and grandmother that I can now. I can't take back any of the mistakes I have made in my past. One of the biggest ones was not taking my daughter, Veronica, with me when I left. I thought that it was what was best for her at the time, and if I had known what I do now, I would have done things so much differently and explained to Adrian that it wasn't her sister's fault for our suffering. It was mine. So God, for that I ask for your forgiveness.

God, cover our daughter, wife, mother, sister, friend, First Lady Veronica and that unborn baby she is carrying. Place your loving arms around her and let her know that you are right there with her.

And God I even pray for all that are involved in this mission that Satan has set up. They may not even realize what they are doing and how they are being used and I pray that you have mercy on them as you see fit. I know he can't do anything without your permission but I also know that no matter what it looks like or how bad it hurts we have to be going through this test right now. Our ways are not like your ways Lord but we trust that your judgment is what's best for her and us all. We just pray that her safe return is in your plans this day.

We thank you right now God for whatever the outcome of this trial is and we will forever give you all of the honor, all of the praise, and all of the glory that you deserve. In your mighty and precious son Jesus' name we pray, Amen." Sarita prayed and I could see how God was removing that weight and burden that she had been feeling all of these years from her.

As everyone cried and hugged one another, Detective Ramos asked me to walk him to the door because there was something that he needed to inform me of away from everyone else.

"What's going on, Detective?" I asked, praying that it wasn't anything bad about my wife.

"When I was on the phone with the station, they informed me that Adrian wanted to speak with you. There are some things that she needs to reveal to you. You don't have to go right now, but when and if you are ready, let me know and I will set up everything," he informed me.

That was the last thing that I expected to hear from him, but I know this was something that needed to be done.

"Set it up for tomorrow afternoon, if you can. The sooner we can get to the bottom of this, the better," I told him, agreeing to meet with her and see what she could possibly have to say to me.

"Lord, I need you to be all up and through this meeting tomorrow, and let your light shine in and on me so that I don't choke the life out of this woman," I said as I closed the door behind him.

"What woman?" I heard MJ ask from behind me.

God knows I didn't want to tell him, but I wouldn't dare lie to him.

"Follow me into my office, son," I simply said before walking away.

Chapter *Fourteen*

Veronica

I don't know how long it had been since my water had broken, and Keith still wouldn't take me to the hospital. All I know is that the sun went down and has risen again. I don't know how much I've dilated, or even if the baby is in the right position to be born. So many things could happen during a home birth, and if the right things weren't set in place, it could be a disaster.

I needed help and I didn't know how much longer I could hang on through these pains. It had been so long since I had kids, so this pain was new all over again. I love me some God, but I swear that when I die and if I make it in, I'm gonna have to sit down with Eve and give her an earful. All this stuff us women went through all because this broad got the munchies!

I was about to laugh at that thought until another contraction hit me like a mac truck.

"OOOOOOOWWWWWWWW!! Keith please helllllllllppp me!" I cried out for the millionth time, but once again, I got no response. I had been in the bed this whole time, but I had to try and get him to take me to the hospital.

I eased out of the bed slowly and made my way over to the door, and started banging as hard as I could to get his attention.

BOOM! BOOM! BOOM! BOOM!

"Keith I need help!!" I screamed, as another pain rocked me from the bottom of my toes all the way up to the top of my head, while the baby kicked me something terrible. I guess he or she was trying to help me bang on the door so we could get out.

"God, please help me. You said you would never leave me. Please God, don't let something happen to this baby or to me before we can get home. Tell me what to do, please," I cried to and begged God all at the same time.

I could feel another contraction about to rock my core again as I grabbed the handle to the door that stayed locked. As soon as the pain started I held on to the knob, but lost my grip and fell as the door unexpectedly opened.

"God, thank you! Keith please help me," I said and realized that no one was on the other side of the door. I did my best to slide as far as I could out of the door and saw nothing but an empty hallway. He must have forgotten to lock it back when I told him my water had broken.

I made my way slowly up the hall, but having to stop through each and every birthing pain I experienced took me way longer than I wanted. I needed to get some help and by the silence I heard throughout the house, I figured I was alone. I didn't know how I was going to get out of here or where Keith was, but one thing I knew was that God was about to show up and show out on our behalf.

I had finally managed to get to the front of the house, and because of the blackout curtains in the living room, I could barely see. I knew it was daytime only by the small window in the room where I had been since I had been taken. It was too high to look out of, but I could see the sky.

It took me a few minutes to find a light switch and turn the lights on. The room was decorated like one of those cover pictures on a *Homes and Gardens* magazine. I hated the way they always looked. It always looked like there was no love or life put into them.

Another contraction hit me as I walked over to the couch. I had to sit down because I was starting to feel so bad. My body was getting heavy and my head was feeling light. I fell back in the seat just as the next contraction started. I knew that I was close to delivering because they were coming back to back now. I looked towards the front door and my hope was almost gone when I saw all of the locks on the door. The way they were positioned, I knew they were only able to be unlocked from the outside. I had no way out until I saw a flashing light come from under the table that sat close to the door.

I tried to make out what it was from where I was sitting, but it was no use. I eased my way over by the door and once I realized what it was, if I wasn't in full blown labor I would have been getting my shout on. Keith had to have been hauling tail out of here because the flashing light was a message indicator on his cell phone!

There was only a two percent battery life left, but all I needed to do was get someone on the phone long enough to get me and my baby some help. I was still feeling dizzy and realized that my baby had all of a sudden stopped kicking. Just as I hit the send button on the phone after dialing 911, I looked over on the sofa where I had previously been and saw a huge red spot. I looked down at my legs and saw blood flowing freely. Before I went down the last thing I saw was the front door opening and hearing, "Hello? Hello? This is 911 what's your

emergency?"

Chapter *Fifteen*

Marcus

After everyone left for the evening and all of the kids were in their rooms tucked away I decided to call it a night. I had to get my mind right for the meeting between Adrian and I in the morning. It took everything in both Malachi and I to calm Torre down when they came to pick up Cadence and Lailani. I messed up and updated them on everything and by the time I was finished Torre was amped up and ready to ride down to the precinct the next day with me.

If I wanted to find out where my wife was I had to be calm and Torre was not bout that like right now. I couldn't deny I though, Torre and Malachi had our backs to the ends of the earth and we had theirs right back.

It was hard to find true friends like that who were really genuine these days. Someone seemed to always want something but not these two. If Veronica and I were up so were they. If we were knocked down they would get right down on that ground and lay beside us until we figured out a way for us all to rise again. It went both ways for us and I couldn't thank God enough for them.

I checked in on the kids to make sure they all had everything they needed for school the next day. When I got to MJ's room I found him in his prayer corner on his knees praying for his mother and unborn sibling. I didn't want to interrupt him but just watching the young man that he was turning into made me happy in spite of all that was going on around us.

I closed his door and made my way to the room that I couldn't wait to share with my wife again. I knew she was coming home and it would be soon. I could feel it deep down in my soul. God was going to bring her and our baby home to us. I wondered if she had even picked out names or if she was waiting to come home so we could name the baby together.

So many thoughts went through my mind as I walked over to our stereo system and began singing along to one of Veronica's favorite songs that seem to be so appropriate right now I thought as I undressed for a shower and got in.

"From now on I'm takin' all it costs

From now on we won't get lost at all

My time is running out, I know

And now I'm tryna restore her hope in me,

Cause clearly, somebody had hurt her

I just wanna be the one who stands

between

Anyone who don't do her right

I'd be there like there tonight

Tryna make this girl see the light

I hope that she sees the love when she

sees me

I hope that she sees all this love I'm

filled with

All I wanna do is, all I wanna do is

Came up with this little plan,

Put her hope back in her man!

I hope that sure she sees the love when

she sees me

I hope that she sees all this love that

we should be

All I wanna do is, all I wanna do is

Came up with this little plan,

Put her hope back in her man."

I stood under that shower head for close to an hour before getting out and heading to bed. I closed my eyes while I listened to the music as it continued to play and pictured that my First Lady was back in my arms again before allowing sleep to take over.

*****

I hadn't realized how late it was until MJ knocked on my door fully dressed, and stated that they were on their way out the door. Malachi was taking the kids to school for me since I had to be down to the station at nine. I looked over and noticed that I only had an hour and a half before I needed to be downtown.

I hurried up and took care of my personal hygiene and dressed in something comfortable. After giving myself the once over, I thought about how each day, no matter what I put on, Veronica made sure to tell me how handsome I looked. I knew my outfit of the day would have been one of her favorites, and I could see the smile forming on her face now as she said, "Mmm mmm mmm" while she licked her lips. I closed my eyes and I swear I could feel her breath on my neck, and then the softness of her lips meeting mine. Opening my eyes, reality brought me back to seeing the reflection of me, rocking a pair of dark blue denim jeans that Veronica bought me, a black bandanna print t-shirt that had a red pocket on the front, and my red low-top Chuck Taylors. In no way was this outfit screaming Pastor, but it was screaming fly, and that is definitely what I was.

I made sure all of the locks were on the doors, as I set the alarm and headed out of the house, hopping in my '71 Chevy Chevelle SS that I bought myself after my last book hit the top of the charts. I was very particular about taking money from the church. I didn't want to be known as one of those pastors who lived high off of the money coming into the church, while my members were struggling. I just didn't see that as being a blessing to the Kingdom, so I made sure that each dollar was put back into the church to help God's people. The blessed life we were living was from the money we made on our own, and God has really increased every area in our lives because of that. My family or our church, never wanted for a thing.

I sent my children a text telling them to have a blessed day, I loved them, and to let the Holy Spirit continue to lead them throughout the day. Once that was done, I pulled out of our driveway and headed to get the information I needed to bring my baby back home. What I didn't know was that the enemy had a few more tricks up his hot sleeves.

Chapter *Sixteen*

Adrian

I was sitting in the visiting room with my lawyer, rubbing my sweaty palms together and waiting on Marcus to get here. I knew there was no turning back now with what I was about to say, but I needed to do this in order to make things right. I knew that I would be going to jail for some time and I needed his help. I just wished the information that I gave would be beneficial and not too little too late.

I hadn't heard from Keith in a few days. The last time I called him, he told me that everything was still going as planned and that he was waiting on me to give him the next steps. I kept stalling because I needed more time to figure out what to do and how to do it so that it would work out in everyone's favor.

Keith didn't know that I was locked up and that Iesha was in a mental hospital. Had he known that, he probably would have panicked and made things worse than they had already were.

"Adrian, are you okay?" my lawyer, Constance, asked me. I knew she was against my decision to speak with Marcus about everything, but no one could stop me from doing this. For once in my life, I was going to correct my mess-ups.

I was about to respond to her, but before I could, the door to the room opened up and in walked Marcus looking like an extra in a music video. I may have been here to make things right, but I was still a woman and this chocolate god in front of me made me have impure thoughts. From the look on Constance's face, she was thinking the same thing I was. This man was F-I-N-E! My sister was a lucky woman indeed.

"Hello Pastor. This is my lawyer, Constance Jordan," I said, trying my best to be professional.

"Adrian. Ms. Jordan," Marcus said while nodding his head and taking a seat at the far end of the table.

"Pastor Millhouse, don't you want to sit a little closer so we can discuss the matter at hand?" Constance asked him.

"No disrespect Ms. Jordan, but if I sit any closer to *Officer* Norman, I may be sporting one of those fresh orange jumpsuits she has on. So it's best that I sit here, if you don't mind," he said, as he talked to her but looked me dead in my face with a look so cold, it was hard to believe that he was a man of the cloth. I guess when you play with people's lives and their families, all things are a go and it's trained-to-go time.

"Pastor, let me start off by saying that I'm sorry for everything," I said.

"As you should be," was his simple, yet slick reply.

I cleared my throat thinking this was about to be harder than I had ever imagined, but knew that I deserved the treatment I was getting. I couldn't blame anyone for this mess but myself. Iesha wasn't even to blame because I had a choice in the matter.

"Keith has my sister, as you may already know," I said.

All he did was nod his head to confirm that he had already known, so I started from the beginning.

Chapter *Seventeen*

Marcus

"I was four years old the first time I remember asking about my father," Adrian started.

"I was playing in my mother's room while she did her friend, Ms. Lillie's hair in the kitchen. That was her hustle when money was low, and she was really good at it. On the days when she had people come over, she would always let me go play dress up in her room so that I would stay out of her way.

That particular day I was in her jewelry box, when I found a picture of her along with a man and another little girl. Instead of waiting until Ms. Lillie left, I ran out of the room yelling,

'Mommy! Mommy! Is this my Daddy?'

I was so excited, but instead of her answering me she gave me one of the coldest stares I had ever seen in my life; one that put some fear in me.

'We will talk about it later,' was all she said.

Even at that young age I knew not to challenge my mother, so I turned around and left the room. For years, neither of us said anything else about him until one day I came home from school. To see my mother lying in the middle of our living room floor, crying and beaten beyond recognition, lit something in me that I never knew I had.

I was so pissed off but so scared at the same time. I didn't know if my mother would make it and if she didn't, what would happen to me? Where would I go? A thirteen year old shouldn't have to think about these things. I was a child and my parents should have been protecting me.

I realized my mother wouldn't be lying in a hospital bed fighting for her life if my father had done right by us. I always thought my mother worked third shift at one of the warehouses downtown, but that was far from the truth. I was watching her suffer all because one of her Johns did this to her."

"Your mother was a prostitute too?" I asked her stunned.

"From the way Sarita and Mrs. Verna explained it to us, the reason she left your father was because she didn't want to be pimped out," I continued.

"Listen. One thing I have learned over time is that a woman will always go back to what she knows, no matter if it's a good thing or something as bad as selling your body. We need to feel that security and if we don't have someone that will provide that for us, we will go out and get it by any means necessary.

My mother didn't want to do it, but when she couldn't afford to feed me or keep clothes on my back, she had to do what she had to do. She finally explained to me that was the reason she left Clarence.

When my mother found out she was pregnant with me, she became scared for not just her life, but mine too. Clarence didn't want children, but when she got pregnant the first time, as soon as he saw Veronica he fell in love with my sister and out of love with our mother. He told her that day after she gave birth that she was lucky he wanted to now keep the baby. But he meant every word he said when he explained if she ever got pregnant again, he would allow her to have it and when she did, she would die right where she lay.

What scared her most was when she heard him say that if she had a girl, that it would become just another one of his hoes. What kind of father would say or do that to one of his children?" Adrian said, before she broke down crying.

I don't care how upset I was with her the God in me wouldn't let me be heartless. Adrian had suffered as a child and young woman, too, and my love for Christ wouldn't allow me to hold hatred in my heart for her.

"Not one Adrian, try both sweetie," I said.

"What do you mean?" she asked me with tears falling down her face. The more I looked at her, the more I saw features that reminded me of Veronica, and I had to look away often. My heart was breaking each second I didn't know where she was.

"I mean that Veronica had to endure pain at the hands of your father too. But because all she knew was her father and what she thought was love from him, she didn't complain. She did everything he asked of her. Even after he died, she continued to be who he wanted her to be instead of who God had called her to be," I let her know.

So many times we compare the pain and struggles that we go through with the next person's, thinking that ours is greater and not realizing that thought the circumstances will be different, but pain was still pain.

I explained to her that if people would just sympathize with others no matter what the situation instead of trying to compete in the game of "Who Hurts More?" we could help each other through it. Often times we let our pain outweigh the feeling we get from the Lord to comfort someone else. In those times, we can be so powerful not only to them, but it will also give us the strength to get through our situation; but that's where we end up missing that test put before us.

It took her a few minutes to gather herself after what I had just revealed before she continued.

"I feel even worse now," she said with her head hung low.

"Adrian, hold your head up. No matter what you have done in life, you always hold your head up high," I said trying my best to encourage her.

"After that day in the hospital with my mother, I vowed to get back at my father and sister. I felt like it was his fault for my mother having to endure what she did and Veronica's fault that he didn't want me. Like, had I been born first I would have had the better life like she did. So I wanted them both to pay," she said, and I saw the fire as well as the deep hurt that was displayed in her eyes.

"Veronica didn't have the better life," I said, trying my best to explain what I could without telling too much. I wanted both Veronica and Adrian to have a face to face so that they each could understand the other's position, but the way things were going I was going to have to air it all out.

"Of course she did!" she yelled, while pounding the table between us hard. It even caused her attorney to jump a little bit.

"It was her that got everything she has always wanted! Our father, the money, freedom from struggling, the husband, the big house, the beautiful kids! I wanted that but she got it!" she continued to yell.

I noticed the guard look in the door and shook my head to let him know that everything was fine. I had to calm her down enough so that she would let us know where my wife was, before the guards decided to take her away.

"Veronica was abused Adrian," I started and noticed the shock on her face.

"What do you mean?" she asked me.

"I wanted this to be a conversation that you had with your sister, but I see now that I need to be the one to tell you this so that you can understand right now.

From the age of seven, your father would have different men but mostly women, doing things to her that no child should have to ever endure. He made her feel like she was the woman of the house because your mother was gone and having that position required her to do things to provide for the household.

Now Clarence never touched Veronica inappropriately, but he never prevented anyone else from doing it. He encouraged it. After each time, he would show her the money that she had made for the family and he would tell her how much he loved her for being a big girl since her mother left them. Never once did he say that he was the cause of Sarita being gone."

"That bastard. How could he do that to her? She was just a little girl. She didn't deserve that," Adrian said.

"As she got older her, heart had gotten so cold against your mother for leaving her to deal with this alone that she wanted to prove to your father that she could be a better woman than Sarita would ever be. So she went harder for Clarence than anyone ever had. By the time she was fifteen, he had her out pimping the same women that abused her as a child, and recruiting new ones. If her father was happy, she was happy," I finished.

"Oh my God. All of this time I helped continue to hurt her because I didn't know the truth. Mrs. Verna told me why my mother left but didn't go into detail. She just said that it was not her or Veronica's fault and she gave me this picture saying that I should tell everything that I know," she said, sliding the picture she had in her lap across to me. It was the one that Mrs. Verna described as she was telling us how she met Sarita for the first time.

"She explained to me that Iesha was sick and manipulated me because she knew that I had an agenda against Clarence and Veronica when I went undercover." That last statement threw me.

"Wait, what? Undercover?" I asked.

"After what my mother told me, I decided to take out my own kind of revenge on the two of them. I continued school so that I could graduate and go off to the police academy. As soon as I graduated, I immediately applied for a position in Chicago. I had done some digging of my own and knew right where they were.

I was working there maybe a year before I was approached by my captain about an assignment that was coming up. He thought I would be a good fit to go undercover to get information about this dude named Bean. I had been doing my homework on the happenings of my father, and knew that he and Bean were at odds.

When I got out on the block, it took me a minute to find out who was who and when I discovered that Iesha was involved with Bean *and* Veronica, I was floored. It wasn't until I got in good with one of the girls named Mimi that she told me what the tea was. Clarence had come in and taken over his side of town with the help of his daughter. They were bringing in more money in a week than Bean had ever seen in a year and he wanted a piece of that. When he went to Clarence to suggest they come together, Clarence laughed in his face and dismissed him. Bean was beyond pissed and felt like Clarence not only disrespected him by taking over his side of town, but then dismissing him like he was the help or something.

You know, when a man already isn't secure in who he is, it takes nothing for someone to crush him further. And it wouldn't be long before he is so bruised that he's coming after any and everybody, especially the ones who hurt him."

I had to agree with her on that one because so many times I saw men come into the church, broken spiritually, and the smallest thing would send them right back to where they had just come from because of hurt. That's why it's so important that we uplift our men and not just black men, all men. Our world is a mess today because our men are not in their rightful positions in God and in their home, I thought to myself.

"So that's what Bean did," Adrian continued.

"The plan was for Iesha to get in good with Veronica and find out all she could and bring the info back to Bean. Once I learned this, every time I saw Iesha come around, I started talking about how much I hated Clarence and I wanted nothing more than to see him suffer.

Eventually we came up with this idea to set up Clarence and take all that he had, but I didn't know that Bean had other ideas for him. I don't care how much I hated him, I never wanted him to die the way he did that night. As I watched him lay on that ground bleeding, I wished I could take it back but it was too late.

Iesha got in my head, reminding me of the reason that we set out to do this and immediately the sadness I felt went away. It was game on. I knew Iesha and Veronica were having an affair, but I thought it was just for us to be able to carry out what we were doing. The feelings I had building up for her were so strong that anything she told me I believed. My judgment was beginning to get cloudy and I didn't see that I was the one really getting played. It didn't matter though, because I knew that we were about to be on top soon.

One day I went in to work and overheard that there was a new investigation into my father's death, so I told Iesha we needed to fall back for a while until things cooled off. I hated that she was always over there with Veronica and I was alone. It started getting to me, so I came up with this BS story that I needed to be taken off of the case because my mother was ill. They approved it and I left Chicago all together and moved to St. Louis." She paused as she winched a little.

"Are you okay Adrian?" her lawyer asked.

"Yes. Yes, I'm okay. I have to get this out now or I never will," she said, looking back at me with a face full of sorrow.

"I tried to keep in touch with Iesha over the next few months, but she was nowhere to be found. After some time I just decided to let it go," she finished.

"I don't get it, though; if you let it go, then why after all of these years did you come back to try and destroy Veronica?" I asked her feeling my pressure begin to rise again.

"I didn't say I let my revenge for Veronica go. I just let looking for Iesha go. Oh, I was still going to make her pay and now I had even more of a reason to. Not only did she cause my mother to leave and my father to not want anything to do with us, she took the woman I had fallen in love with too," she said, stopping abruptly and doubling over in what I was sure was pain.

Before anyone had time to tell one of the guards to get help, the door opened and in rushed Detective Ramos.

"We found Veronica!" he said out of breath.

"WHAT! WHERE IS SHE?" I yelled, jumping up while praying the love of my life was alive.

"We just got a call from University of Chicago Medical Center saying that Veronica was brought in and dropped off by an unknown male. When asked who he was, he left as fast as he came without giving any information. From the description we got, it sounds a lot like Officer Keith Washington."

"Is she okay? Please tell me she's okay," I said, almost begging him at the same time.

"So far she's okay. The doctors said when she came to all she could mutter was to call her husband. She had enough strength to give the house number and it was intercepted by the wire taps we had placed in your home. One of my men called me right away with the information and I knew you were still here. We have to go, though. Veronica's in labor," he said filling us in.

"So is Adrian! Get her some help; this baby is coming now!" her lawyer said.

The what?! Please God, no. This can't be my life, I thought as I was ushered out of the room and to an awaiting squad car outside.

Chapter *Eighteen*

Veronica

When I get home, Marcus better not ever touch me again! This pain was nothing like I remembered, or maybe it was just intense because I didn't have him here with me to help me deal with the discomfort. Either way I was ready for this baby to be out.

I was scared and thankful at the same time when I came to in the labor and delivery room. The last thing I remembered was hearing the 911 operator and the front door to where I was being held coming open. I knew that I had to let someone know to get my husband, and all I could get out was his name and our home number. Our connection was so strong I knew that someone would be there.

Apparently, Keith just dropped me off and left. I guess he did have a little sympathy for me and my baby after all. It was comforting to know that the blood I saw didn't mean our baby was in any danger. I had a cyst that I didn't know about because I hadn't had any prenatal visits, so when I fell the fall caused it to rupture. I was just glad nothing was seriously wrong.

The doctor in charge of my care was pleased to let me know that even with no care, our baby boy was just fine, as was I. Now all I needed was to see the faces of my husband and our other children. The more I thought of seeing them again, the more I praised God for keeping us safe and bringing them back to me.

"Baby!" I heard, and I broke down crying as I looked over to the door and saw the smiling and crying face of the one and only man who to this day has never hurt me.

"Marcus," I said barely above a whisper, as this contraction started to rock my body. As soon as I closed my eyes to brace myself, I felt his hand grab mine and it seemed as if all of the pain I had been feeling was taken away.

"God I thank you," was all that he kept repeating, as he kissed my lips for the first time in seven months, and rubbed his hand across my swollen belly. As soon as he put his hand there, it was like our child knew his daddy was here and immediately started kicking again.

"It's a boy," I said smiling, knowing that he had always wanted another son. He always felt like he was out numbered and when we learned that MJ was expecting a girl, he was really outnumbered. Thinking of our grandchild and our kids, it was like Marcus could read my mind as he said, "They are all outside. I didn't know what kind of shape you would be in and I didn't want them to see you any other way than the last time they saw you," he said, as he kissed me again and walked back over to the door.

"MOMMY!" my kids squealed, as I broke down seeing the faces that I missed so much. Entering heaven couldn't feel any better than what I was feeling right now, having my family back in my arms.

"Hey my pudd!" I heard coming from my left, as the kids moved and I saw my best friend Torre running towards me.

"My pudd!" I said back to her. That was our little nickname that we had for one another. I forgot what reality show we got that from, but it stuck with us.

"I'm so glad you are okay. I missed you so much! Did that nigga hurt you? Wait til I find him. I got a hot one waiting on him when I do. Your sister is lucky Marcus wouldn't let me go with him to the jailhouse to see him, or she would have caught the first one," Torre ranted on and spilled the beans all at the same time.

This woman couldn't hold a cup of water in a desert if she tried, but we loved her just the same.

"Sister?" I said confused.

"Baby, let's just get our son here safely before we discuss everything. I have you back now and I don't want to think about anyone else right now. God has truly been a miracle worker," my husband said. I agreed for now, but he was gonna tell me what was going on soon.

Before I could say anything else, I heard a baby cry. I looked around the room and landed on my first baby holding his first baby. The water works started again, as he handed me my first grandchild.

"She's gorgeous MJ. She looks just like you and Lailani," I said, as I looked down into her beautiful face as she stopped crying. It looked like she was examining me because I was a new face, and it was like at that moment she knew I was her grandmother and broke out into a toothless smile.

"She knows who you are," Lailani said to me as she hugged me and kissed the top of my head.

"Her name is Cadence," MJ told me.

I looked up at him and laughed. "You always liked that name and said when you grew up and had a daughter, God told you her name was going to be Cadence," I said as he smiled wide. He was a proud father, and I knew because he had the perfect example of what a father is, Cadence had nothing to worry about. Her life would be a good one.

I was just about to say something else when I got the urge to use the bathroom. I may not have remembered this pain but I remembered what this feeling meant.

Chapter *Nineteen*

Marcus

It was show time.

"Marcus, get the doctor. I have to push!" Veronica said handing my little Cadence to her mother, but not before giving her another kiss on her fat cheek.

Everyone left the room as the doctor rushed in dressed for the occasion.

"Mr. Millhouse, you might want to put this on as fast as you can so you don't mess up your clothes," he said as the nurse handed me a set of scrubs.

"Please hold on until I change, baby. I have never missed any of our kids being born and I don't plan on doing it now," I said as I kissed her.

"I know that and you know that, but our baby has no idea. He's ready to meet the man he's heard about for the last few months," she replied smiling.

I ran off into the bathroom and knew I didn't have enough time to fully change, so I just pulled the uniform over my own clothes and hurried out.

"Alright Veronica, with this next contraction I want you to push as hard as you can," Dr. Warren instructed her.

I made the mistake once again, of giving her my hand to hold. During each labor I had given her my hand to hold, and she brought me to tears. My wife wasn't the smallest woman and she was by far the biggest, but the strength she had in the time of pain baffled me. I couldn't let go even if I wanted to.

Forty-five minutes and many pushes later, God allowed our youngest son, Christian Immanuel Millhouse, to enter the world.

"I can't believe we just had another baby," I said, as I held our son close to my heart.

"Are you okay with it? I mean, I know that we didn't plan this," Veronica asked me.

"Our ways are not like God's ways and our thoughts are not His. But in the end, they all work out for our good and I'm so grateful to Him that He has blessed us with this gift and bringing you back to us unharmed," I said to her, as I sat on the bed and kissed her as deeply as I could. I wanted her to feel the deepest part of my soul and know that now that I had her back, I was never letting her go.

"Uh, isn't that how you got this baby?" we heard Destiny say as she and her sister cracked up.

"I would tell you to get you some biz-ni-ee, but because I'm in such a happy place I'm gonna let that comment slide this time," I said laughing along with them. I finally had my whole family back and nothing was going to take that away from me.

If there is one thing I learned throughout life, when you experience the good, be prepared for the ugly head of the enemy to try and throw a monkey wrench in the mix. Of course I knew that something would rear its ugly head sooner or later; I just hoped it was the later. But with the way things had been set up in my life these days, I knew trouble was about to hit.

Just as I was about to say a prayer for our family, there was a knock at the door. Everyone was already in the room including the doctor, so I had no idea who it could have been. Malachi was the closest to the door and the look on his face after he opened it confirmed that some more mess was about to hit the fan.

He slowly moved away from the door and entered Veronica's mother, Sarita. I had been so focused on getting here as fast as I could from Atlanta that it never crossed my mind to find out where Sarita or Iesha's parents had gone. I just knew I had to get to my wife.

The closer she got to the bed, it seemed like everyone had been holding their breaths because none of us knew how this reunion would go. I looked at Veronica and saw that once the recognition flashed across her face, things were about to go left real quick.

Before Veronica could utter a word, her mother spoke first.

"Veronica, I apologize for everything that happened in your life. I now know how my actions hurt you, even though I thought I was protecting you. I never knew that your father would hurt you so much, and I don't think I will ever forgive myself for this pain. But I pray that you can find it in your heart to forgive me. I not only caused you harm, but your sister as well. I want the two of you to eventually find a common ground before I leave this earth. I want to know that my girls are in each other's lives the way it should have been from the beginning," Sarita poured out her emotions during this plea.

I don't think anyone was breathing and when Veronica finally spoke for the first time, I knew everyone in there had died because I was having an out of body experience.

"I can forgive you mother," she said, sounding so cold that the hair on the back of my neck stood at attention and my arms filled with goose bumps.

"Thank you baby," Sarita said, not picking up on the same thing that I did. Something was terribly wrong.

"But what I won't do is forgive your trifling daughter, Adrian. It's one thing to drug my husband and then seduce him, but it is something totally different when she doesn't even consider using a condom to prevent herself from getting pregnant by him. She should be going into labor any day now, right Mommy

Dearest?" she ended, causing my world to stop

yet again.

To be continued……

CPSIA information can be obtained at www.ICGtesting.com
Printed in the USA
LVOW06s2136260715

447744LV00008B/97/P